# my saucy
# stuffed ravioli

**Also by Cherry Whytock**

*My Cup Runneth Over*

*My Scrumptious Scottish Dumplings*

# my saucy stuffed ravioli

## the life of Angelica Cookson Potts

# Cherry Whytock

Simon & Schuster Books for Young Readers
New York  London  Toronto  Sydney

SIMON & SCHUSTER BOOKS FOR YOUNG READERS
An imprint of Simon & Schuster Children's Publishing Division
1230 Avenue of the Americas, New York, New York 10020
This book is a work of fiction. Any references to historical events,
real people, or real locales are used fictitiously. Other names, characters,
places, and incidents are products of the author's imagination, and any
resemblance to actual events or locales or persons,
living or dead, is entirely coincidental.

Library of Congress Cataloging-in-Publication Data
Whytock, Cherry.
My saucy stuffed ravioli : the life of Angelica Cookson Potts / Cherry
Whytock.
p. cm.
Summary: While preparing for and going on vacation to Italy with her
friends and family, food-loving English teenager Angelica deals with her
unrequited love for Sydney, her fear of being seen in public in a bikini, and
her worries that her mother might be having an affair. Includes recipes.
ISBN-13: 978-0-689-86550-3
ISBN-10: 0-689-86550-3
[1. Interpersonal relations—Fiction. 2. Vacations—Fiction. 3. Cookery—Fiction.
4. England—Fiction. 5. Italy—Fiction. 6. Humorous stories.] I. Title.
PZ7.W6246Mys 2006
[Fic]—dc22     2005051568

For Jens, Peter and St. Joan,
with a bow and a rose

## chapter one

# Balloons, Buffoons, Banners, and Babes

"SO TELL US some more about your week. Was it really wicked and wonderful?" asks Minnie as she pins our brilliant *Welcome Back!* sign across the hallway. We've written it using all the "pulsating" pink lipsticks I don't like anymore.

"Well, yes . . ." I say, "but I just kept thinking about *him*." I pull in my stomach and suck in my cheeks, hoping that I might look lovesick (although I don't think I've changed much over the last week).

My heart just kept belly-flopping around the whole week I spent doing Work Experience at Greatsnott Manor. I couldn't seem to concentrate on anything Mr. Dreamy Dimples asked me to do. . . .

"Crumbs, Minnie, I AM SO IN LOVE. . . . Love has come along and swept me up in his tanned, muscular ar—"

"Yes, yes," says Portia in between puffing up balloons, "but tell me this: Did you learn to make delish new dishes or did you just moon around over the mixer? What was the *Work Experience* like? Was the chef—whatever you call him . . .

Mr. Dreamy Dimples—as dreamy as you remembered him?"

Mr. Dreamy Dimples is the Chef at Greatsnott Manor Health Spa, where Mother dragged me during the Easter break. Apart from being allowed to help Mr. Dreamy Dimples in the kitchen, it was completely horrible—especially as Potty was nearly taken off to prison while we were there. He'd been banging on about a "haggis hoax" in Harrods and the owner of Harrods, Mr. Alfie Highead, wasn't at ALL pleased—that is, until he discovered that Potty was right, there *was* something fishy going on. Since then, Mr. Highead can't do enough for Potty, which is why he gave us all a free week at Greatsnott as a thank-you and is lending us his villa in Italy during summer holidays. Mother and Potty loved every minute at the health spa and kept going on about Alfie Highead's lavish generosity. I didn't want to do that embarrassing massage and beauty treatment bit again, so I spent my time doing Work Experience in the kitchen, which was fine by me.

To be honest, I don't remember much

Minnie chopped these short for me—so this season

pink to-die-for snakeskin

2

about either Mr. Dreamy Dimples or my Work Experience, even though we only got back from Greatsnott yesterday. I do remember that Mr. Dreamy Dimples told me that the best way to a man's heart was through his stomach. (I think that was after I had confided in him that I couldn't possibly chop up the carrots he had given me because something about them reminded me of my beloved SYDNEY.)

The girlies get tired of waiting for me to answer. "Where shall we hang the balloons?" asks Minnie as she staggers around the room with them, looking like an overgrown pink raspberry.

somewhere behind these balloons is Minnie, all blonde and curvy and cutie-pie

Portia puffing herself pink

has been known to stuff her bra with toilet paper

NEVER GETS ANY FATTER!

flowers sewn on by Minnie

uses antiseptic wipes on

her shoes— freak!

often on tiptoe— says she's "vertically challenged" (teeny- weeny)

"Put them somewhere out of Angel's reach," says Portia, "so she can't go painting hearts on them like she has with everything else around here."

"I must say, Angel," says Minnie, as she tries to loop some balloons over the light fixture and misses, because even on tippy-toe she's minute, "you've certainly changed your tune about Sydney."

"I know, I was mad . . ." I sigh, reaching up over her head to fix the balloons. As soon as I kissed him for the first time, I just KNEW he was the only one for me.

"I sleep with the handles of the Harrods bag he held under my pillow."

There's something about the way that Portia and Minnie look at each other that I think I'll ignore. What do *they* know of LOVE? What does *anyone* know of my grand passion?? How could they understand that that first kiss was like everything delicious all at once . . . like JONC's (Jamie Oliver, Naked Chef and Divine Superstar's) most scrumptious chocolate pots with whipped cream and possibly Mars Bar sauce on top. Sydney would never give me one of those sucky slobbery kisses that make a squelching noise when they finish. His kisses are like fairy cakes and icing sugar with the softest meringue moment at the end . . .

Actually, to be perfectly honest, ever since I decided that Sydney was the one for me, there hasn't been that much action on the passion front. I think he's probably spellbound by my total gorgeousness and tongue-tied with emotion whenever he sees me, but it is a teeny bit upset-making that I can count his meringue-flavored kisses on the fingers of one hand . . . *and* that there WASN'T a passionate letter waiting for me when I got home . . .

"I can't believe Mr. Highead is letting us all stay with you in his villa in Italy—it is going to be totally fantastic," says Portia, breaking my train of thought.

"I really hope Mercedes can come too. OOOOh, it's so exciting!" squeaks Minnie.

Somehow we've got to convince Mercedes's grandparents it's a good idea for her to go away again so soon after getting back from America. They love her to pieces, so I'm pretty sure they'll want her to do whatever makes her happiest.

"Dahlings, how colorful," says Mother as she wafts downstairs in head-to-toe Gucci. "What a heavenly surprise for dear Mercedes! When is it that she's due back?" she asks, squinting at our awesome artwork. Mother will never admit to needing specs ("Spectacles are just so *senior*, dahling").

Mother doesn't usually "do" excited as she thinks *any* emotion is aging, but even she is showing signs of excitement—although she's too thin to get properly excited about anything. I mean, anyone who thinks a stick of celery and a cup of

"pearls, dahling" and the only bit of this outfit that would fit round any bit of me

just enough space in here for sixteen credit cards and her perfect pout, liposome-rich, collagen-coated, pink petunia lipstick

**Mother, mid-waft**

5

black coffee can be called lunch has to be halfway insane. There is no way anyone could have enough energy with that sort of lunch inside them to do anything more exciting than wafting about a bit, which, actually, is what Mother does most of the time. I often wonder whether I am truly her daughter. I mean, how come I got to be so . . . so . . . well, so STRAPPING, when she's so spaghetti skinny? Sometimes she looks at me as if she can't believe it either. How did her little minnow's body produce a walloping whale like me? Whenever I help myself to extra pasta, she gives me one of those "looks" that say all sorts of things like, "Should you really be eating that when the seams of your jeans need counseling?" or, "Don't you think fewer potatoes would be a good idea when all your zips need stress management?"

Most of the time I don't care, though. There's almost nothing as fab as food. (There's Sydney, obviously, but covering him with chocolate fudge icing and serving him up to my friends wouldn't really be quite right, would it?) *Food* can be shared with all the people you love and makes everyone (except Mother) feel warm and happy and NOT HUNGRY.

Thank God Flossie was around to teach me to cook. Flossie's the sort of yummy mummy that Mother could never be. Of course, she's not my mother, she's our housekeeper, but she's the one who used to read me *Winnie-the-Pooh* when I was little. She's the one who gives me Syrup of Figs when she thinks I look peaked (although I wish she wouldn't—it tastes DISGUSTING and has the most disastrous effects in the bathroom department).

Mother spent most of her time at Greatsnott reading Italian

*Vogue*—or rather, looking at the pictures and saying everything was *bella*. In fact, she's been positively cheerful these days. Yes, something very odd has happened to Mother recently. Whereas she used to waft about doing absolutely NOTHING but be pampered and spend money, now she wafts about as if she's got Things to Do and Places to Go. She even dares to risk *smiling* sometimes, which is very out of character.

"Her grandparents are collecting her from the airport tomorrow at ten," I tell her, getting back to thinking about Mercedes, "and they've promised to drop in on their way home. We thought we could give them all lunch."

"Dahling," says Mother, losing interest at the mention of food, "have you seen Potty?"

"I think he's gone to Harrods," (our local "corner store"—a minute away as the crow flies, although you don't see many crows in Knightsbridge). "He said that Alfie had asked his opinion on some bird's nest soup they've just got in." (Maybe the crow's flying there to ask for his nest back.)

"Ah," says Mother without much enthusiasm. "I've just got to pootle off for a teeny while, dahlings. If he comes back and asks where I am, tell him I'm having my nails done."

"Oh, okay," I say, glancing at Mother's strawberry-colored nails, which already look immaculate.

"And if you see George, dahling," she adds as she wafts toward the front door, "tell him that his ticket arrived this morning and I've put it in Potty's office for safe keeping."

I catch Minnie's eye when Mother mentions George. A long time ago George told me that he fancied me, which, as I

7

explained to him, was quite RIDICULOUS—I mean, he's like a brother. I think he's over it now, although he's made it pretty obvious that he doesn't think much of Sydney. But my love life is none of his business. Before I left for my Work Experience, Minnie and George had a sort of "thing" going.

"It's all right, Angel," Minnie says, "I'm so over him. He was just too Strong and Silent—it made me really nervous . . . But . . ." she says with a bashful flutter that looks maddeningly cute on her sweet little blonde-framed face, "I did think George's friend Jimmie was so totally pukka." *Pukka* is a word we girlies have adopted from JONC, Superstar, MBE (More Beautiful than Ever) —it means *GORGEOISE*.

"George is taking Jimmie on holiday with him."

"Oh," says Minnie, looking crestfallen. "Will they be away long?"

"About a month, I think," I tell her, trying to look sympathetic. But really, what could Minnie know of true love and longing? How could her crush on Jimmie possibly compare with my love for Sydney?

"Heavens to Betsy!" we hear Flossie squawk from the basement. "Look what that dog's gone and done now!"

BIG knickers

Stinker

"What has Stinker done, Flossie?" I call down the stairs.

"He's only gone and burrowed into next door's garden again and . . . oh, lawks—he must have savaged the clothesline. He's got what looks like a pair of knickers hanging out of his mouth!"

8

## chapter two

# Gorgeous, Greasy Greetings

OOOH . . . WOE IS ME and ENORMOUS SOBS! I didn't see Sydney in my dreams last night and I was trying *so* hard. Instead I dreamed that my wobble factor had got so humungous that I couldn't squodge out of the door of Heaven (my top-floor bedroom) and that Mrs. Sophie Something-Hyphenated (our next door neighbor and owner of the clothes-line) wasn't able to take me to school in her revolting Range Rover, so I couldn't see Sydney AT ALL. And I knew in my dream that he was missing me dreadfully, because I'd been away all week doing my Work Experience . . . I felt just so desperate that I woke up feeling really, really hungry and I had to have two homemade croissants and a bowl of Flossie's munchy muesli just to stop me from feeling faint. (I know that no matter how hard I try, I'll never manage to faint, but I think I could easily *swoon*, which sounds every bit as interesting.)

Minnie and Portia stayed the night just in case Mercedes's flight came in early. As they were still fast asleep, and as I hadn't heard from Sydney, I sat down and wrote him a long, newsy, passionate letter which I may pop into his locker on Monday morning along with a few of my famous heart-shaped biscuits all tied up with pink tissue paper and maybe a big red bow. The few times I called him from Greatsnott he never really said anything—mostly he just sort of grunted in a very UNromantic way. But it's okay, because I know that some people just aren't any good on the telephone.

a totally potty pamphlet

mmmarmite

red and white striped pajama trousers— his favorite

**Potty**

Flossie gave him these for his birthday—they reminded her of Stinker

Anyway, it's late Sunday morning and Minnie, Portia, and I are standing around in the hall sort of jittering and tweaking our decorative delights. In between jittering and tweaking, we run up and down the stairs to the basement to check that all the food Flossie and I made yesterday for lunch is as amazing as we think it is.

Honestly, my nerves are in shreds! It's bad enough waiting to see one of my best, best friends after being apart for *ages* without the added anxiety of waiting for Sydney to call.

Potty and Stinker are not helping my nerves one bit. Potty keeps bounding out of the study and shouting things like, "Ah ha! I knew I was right!

Absolutely no action on the welcome front yet."

He's working on another of his pamphlets, "The Magic of Marmite." "Full of health-giving Vitamin B, Cherub. Makes your hair shine and your skin glow."

Honestly, you'd think he'd just invented the icky black stuff, he's so excited about it. "Alfie's asked me to research the culinary possibilities of Marmite. Seems they might do a promotion for it in The Store." ("The Store" is what Potty calls Harrods now. I think he feels that it is as much his shop as Alfie Highead's. I suspect Alfie's just asked Potty to do the Marmite research to keep him out of mischief.)

Obviously Potty is completely potty. He's much too ancient to work now—although he used to be a seriously clever barrister. In fact, he's so old that it's more like living with a grandfather than a father. But it does have some advantages—for example, he's way too old to tell me off properly, and because he doesn't work, he's always around and he's got lots of time to sit and chat, which can be really lovely.

"Did you know, little Cherub, that you can spread it on *pommes frites* as a splendiferous and scrumptious treat?"

Marmite and chips—oh yummy (not). But as I love Potty to pieces and he looks so excited about his discovery I just say, "Wow! Now that is truly amazing." Which makes him look terribly chuffed.

"So," says Minnie, stifling a giggle as Potty shuffles back into his study, "did Potty and your mother enjoy themselves at Greatsnott?"

"Potty thought it was the 'hottest thing since fresh toast.'"

11

He spent most of his time in the Turkish baths discussing haggis with anyone who would listen."

"Yuck!" says Portia. "Hasn't he had enough of haggis?"

"Potty could never have enough haggis, and since the Harrods haggis fiasco, he and Alfie Highead have become best, best mates. Alfie asks Potty's opinion about *all* the food in Harrods these days."

Stinker, who has been hurtling around the hall, has now stopped dead in his tracks under the balloons, which he's gazing at with a wicked glint in his eye.

"Do you think they'll be much longer?" sighs Minnie, as she lures Stinker away from the balloons with the promise of a "biccy", which she doesn't actually have. So cruel . . .

All this waiting around for Mercedes to arrive or for Sydney to call is beginning to drive me BATTY. . . .

To pass the time, Portia starts asking math whiz kid Minnie to do some very boring calculations involving a list that she's made about baggage reclaim, the number of passengers, and the length of the journey from the airport to here.

AAAARGH! I think I might scream. . . .

"Oh, for goodness' sake!" I say. "Let's just run downstairs again and make sure that the Slow-Cooked and Stuffed Red Peppers are as 'blinding' as JONC says they ought to be."

I need something, anything, to pass the time and running up and down the stairs is at least good for lowering the wobble factor (which doesn't seem to have gone down at all, despite all my pining for Sydney and the yoga classes I managed to fit in at Greatsnott)—even if the pounding on the stairs does make Mother shout at us to go *più tranquillo*, dahlings!" (which means what, exactly?) before she wafts out of the front door. Mother *does* seem to be spending a lot of time being "out" and "busy" these days. Normally she can go for days on end just lying around having people come and give her "treatments" (i.e., things to make her look less ancient). Oh well, it's great that whatever it is that she's doing seems to be keeping her spirits up for a change.

"Angelica Cookson Potts!" screeches Flossie. "What *are* you doing, may I ask, young lady?"

new hairdo—she calls the little curl on her forehead a "kiss-curl" (sweet)

something yummy-scrummy

somewhere nearby there will be a bottle of Syrup of Figs

**Flossie**

"Oops, sorry, Flossie," I say, licking my finger clean. "I was checking to make sure that Jamie's malt ball ice cream is as 'pukka' as it should be—and," I add quickly, "there's nothing to worry about—it is!"

I can see that Portia is just about to make some comment about germs and hygiene, which she is heavily into, and I'm getting ready to tell her that Mr. Dreamy Dimples says that every good chef tastes her own food, all the time, when the doorbell rings!

"It's HER!" I shout. "They're HERE! Quick, everyone, upstairs and into your positions . . ."

We hurtle up the stairs, leaping nimbly over Stinker on the way, and arrange ourselves in order of height (*à la* family von Trapp) in the hallway before Flossie puffs up the stairs behind us and opens the front door.

As soon as our long-lost, beautiful friend (and her grand-parents) are through the door, I forget about Sydney and we start the routine from *Grease* that we've been practicing since the moment we found out Mercedes was coming home.

We were supposed to do a groovy little dance routine. I'm meant to do a sort of slouchy strut like Rizzo does, while Minnie and Portia do a bit of that rock-and-roll thing that Olivia Newton-John and John Travolta do. Mercedes is standing stock-still, as: (a) my slouchy thing goes wrong and turns into more of a giggly wobble, and (b) Minnie completely loses the plot and rushes at the rather worried-looking Mercedes to give her a great big hug. Of course Portia and I have to abandon our brilliant performance and do the same.

"OOOOOOH," we squeal in unison. "OOOOOOH, it's SOOOO-OOO good to have you back! OOOOOOH, we've missed you SOOOOOO much you just wouldn't believe!!!" And then there's loads of kissing and hugging and saying, "Hi!" to Mercedes's fabby grandparents before Potty arrives and takes them off into the drawing room for "a little snifter" before lunch.

Mercedes looks divine as usual. She hasn't put on an ounce

Mercedes's hair—I WANT IT!

new beaded belt
—bought in Florida

Mercedes's
knickers (crumbs!!)

**Mercedes**

and her wicked wild hair is even longer and wilder than it was before she left.

"Tell us *all* about it," we all beg.

"Well," she begins, with just the hint of an American accent, "some of it was fairly gross," (with more than a hint of the old Americano this time). "You would not believe some of the kids in my school. They were, like, so far out it wasn't for real. There was this one kid who used to, like, wear all his clothes back-to-front because he said it made him feel like he had eyes in the back of his head . . . like, WEIRD!"

"Goodness!" I say, somehow sounding exactly like Miss Upper-Class Twit of the Year. I wish I had a cool accent like Mercedes. She sounds way more US of A than she did when I last spoke to her. I wonder whether Sydney would be more responsive if I had a cool American accent. I decide to listen to her every word and try my best to sound like her . . . like.

"But were they all, like, weird?" I ask, trying a little twang at the end of my question.

Mercedes raises her eyebrow a bit before answering. "No way. Some of those guys were, like, so cooo-el. I really had a ball with them."

"Oh, like . . ." I say, feeling really put out that Mercedes had "a ball" with anyone other than us. I mean, I didn't want her to have a horrible time or anything, I just didn't want her to have as nice a time with them as she has with us.

"Great, like," says Portia.

"Like, wow, like," says Minnie in between giggles.

Even Mercedes is giggling now. "Oh, it's okay. I can tell you there was not one single kid there who was anything like as bodacious as you guys."

"Oh, like, good," I say, and Minnie and Portia echo the word "like" in between giggles. But I'm wondering if it is good to be bodacious.

"And just to, like, show y'all how much I love you, I've brought you each a gift from fabulous Florida."

I'm about to feel upset again about Florida being fabulous when Mercedes produces this wicked-looking thing from her carrier bag. "This is for you, Angel," she says. "It's an Angel

17

Food Cake tin. I saw it and I thought, like, Angel's just gotta have THAT!"

I'm all choked up (like). "That is such a lovely present. And I never knew there was a cake named after *moi*! I shall make Sydney an Angel Food Cake . . . except I'm not sure how to do it."

"I thought of that," says Mercedes, digging into the depths of her bag. "Here. I copied this recipe especially for you. So how is everything with Sydney?"

"Terrific!" I say, hoping that I'm right.

"I'm so happy for you, Angel. Like, I always thought it would work out great for you guys."

"Well, to be perfectly honest . . ." I begin, but before I can explain that Sydney hasn't exactly been as captivating as he might have been in the cupid department, and that he still hasn't called me, even though I've been back from Greatsnott for more than a whole day already, Mercedes pulls another interesting package out of her bag.

"Oh, sorry, wrong package," she says as she flings a pair of minute "underpinnings" back into her bag.

"No, let's have a look," I say and the three of us gaze in won-derment at this whisper of T-shaped lace that's apparently a pair of underpants. Ow, I think. She digs around in her bag again.

She has chosen seriously good presents for each of us. There are some "awesome" hair-grip things for Minnie, all sparkly and funky. And for Portia there is a set of divine gel pens and incredibly pretty paper to make her endless lists on. We all have to hug Mercedes again and GOSH, it is so good to have her here.

"Are you coming back to school until the end of term?" asks Portia, ever the practical one.

"Yup, I think so," Mercedes answers. "They thought it would be easier for me to integrate if I, like, popped in for a day or two."

"Lucky you!" I say with sophisticated sarcasm.

"Oh," says Minnie, "does that mean you'll be here for Sports Day?"

"Probably," says Mercedes.

"Lucky, lucky you!" I say, meaning it *not one bit*—except that for Mercedes, actually, School Sports Day is not the Cruel Shorts Day that it is for some of us.

While we are discussing the special torture of sport, Flossie waddles up from the kitchen and tells us that she has decided that we should eat in the dining room as it is a special occasion. This is a good idea, I suppose, except that the dining room is up here on the ground floor and not in the cozy basement (which I love—it always smells of delish baking or newly ironed laundry).

After we have carted all the goodies upstairs Mother drifts in, back from wherever she's been and graces us with her company.

I have to hand it to her (no, not the lunch, of which she eats almost nothing), she is a brilliant hostess. You can see she makes Mercedes's grandparents feel really at home. By the end of the meal Mercedes's granny, who is Spanish—part of the reason Mercedes is so exotic-looking (the other part being that her father is Jamaican) shows us how they do things in Spain and we finish our pudding (malt ball ice cream and almond *tuiles*—a posh name for thin biscuits) with something called a fandango around the dining room table. Even Mother joins in with the heel clacking and the hand clapping. But then Minnie notices that poor Mercedes is nodding off in her chair with her elbow in the butter dish.

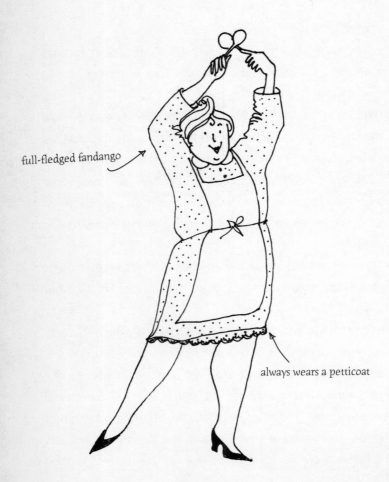

full-fledged fandango

always wears a petticoat

# Crunchy, Munchy, Mouth-Watering Malt Ball Ice Cream

*Really posh (if poss) vanilla ice cream*
*Loadsa malt balls*

---

Put the malt balls in a plastic bag (bigger than the one they come in). Make sure the bag is tightly closed, then crush the malt balls using a rolling pin.

Scoop blobs of ice cream into a bowl and sprinkle on the crunched up pieces of malt balls.

That's it . . . Oh, and then you eat it!

You could try the same scrunching technique with chocolate-covered ginger biscuits for a slightly more sophisticated taste sensation.

## chapter three

# Crumbling Cookies and Castanets

"**WHY DON'T YOU** show George how to do the fandango, Flossie?" I say after we have finished washing up. George is leaning against the dresser looking Strong and Silent, just back from a friend's house where they've been discussing what will happen if they fail all their exams.

Flossie is surprisingly eager to show off her newfound skill and she whisks up two of her wooden spoons to use as castanets. Having Mercedes here has *almost* taken my mind off Sydney.

Mercedes's grandparents have taken her home for a good sleep. Minnie and Portia also went home, after helping Flossie and me take all the dirty dishes back down to the kitchen. Mother and Potty are in the drawing room listening to opera (at least I think they are—I can hear Potty singing).

Flossie gets to the bit where she's supposed to shout "*olé*," which you pronounce "oh lay" (sounds like the sort of thing you might say to a constipated hen), and it's just so sweet to see Flossie prancing about being a Spanish flamingo dancer (or is it a flamenco?), I have to "tra la la" along and do a bit of encouraging hand clapping. But when I look across at George, he's just standing there like a Doric column with a stony look on his face.

"Like, what's up, George?" I finally ask, practicing my drop-dead, fascinating American accent. He's so obviously trying to look put upon that I feel it would be mean not to notice. Flossie stops prancing mid-twirl and straightens her apron.

"Oh, nothing," he sighs, so obviously meaning *everything*.

"Lawks!" puffs Flossie, putting her castanets back in the spoon drawer. "You young people just don't know you're born. When I was young we all knew which side our bread was buttered on," which is one of those Flossyisms that probably has got some deep meaning, but just at the moment I don't think that either George or I know what it might be. (She says so many odd things. She calls my parents Mr. and Mrs. Seepy, for example—Seepy as in CP, Cookson Potts.)

"Yeah, like, right, Flossie," I say, chewing on imaginary gum (which is SO coo-el). "So, like, George, what is it?"

"Well, you wouldn't understand, Angel, especially now that you seem to have developed a brain malfunction that's making you say 'like,' all the time."

The trouble with George is that he knows me *too well*. I mean he's spent most of his school life with us because his parents live abroad.

"Oh, all right," I say, reverting to upper-class-twit accent (I shall practice the drop-dead, fascinating American twang in the privacy of Heaven later on). "What's wrong, then?"

George then blahs on a bit about how CRUCIAL all his

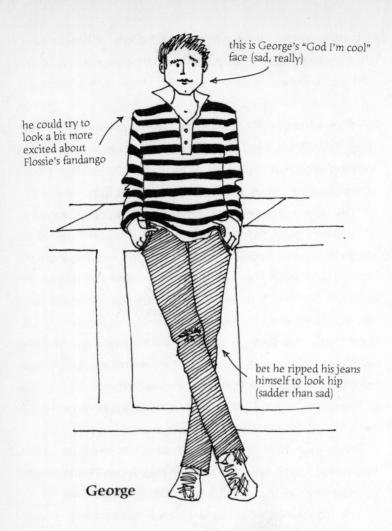

this is George's "God I'm cool" face (sad, really)

he could try to look a bit more excited about Flossie's fandango

bet he ripped his jeans himself to look hip (sadder than sad)

**George**

exams are and how no one could possibly know the awfulness of A-levels and how the bottom will fall out of his world if he doesn't do really well. He goes on for so long (this is something he's started doing these days, which is odd as he used to not speak much at all) that Flossie decides he must need a dose of Syrup of Figs. I can't help pointing out to him that the bottom may not drop out of his world, but if he lets Flossie give him her evil dose, the world will certainly drop out of his bottom, but George doesn't think that's at all funny.

Flossie abandons the Syrup of Figs idea because George gathers up enough strength to say, "NO!" loudly when she produces the bottle and he's much bigger than she is. We do our best to cheer George up. He has, after all, finished his exams now and he's just about to go west to the Indies and that doesn't seem too dreadful to me. I, on the other hand, have to go back to school and face the prospect of humungous humiliation on Cruel Shorts Day and the awful possibility that Sydney may see me in my all-too-revealing sports gear. Crumbs. I don't think I can let my mind go there. I shall have to spend every spare minute at the gym doing kickboxing and yoga.

We make George a tempting plate full of leftovers, as food usually makes him feel better. He can't have any of the malt ball ice cream, though, as I have very helpfully already finished it. (Well, you can't put ice cream back in the freezer when it's turned into gloop, can you?)

As he's noshing away, Mother shouts, "See you later!" from the hall and slams the front door. Where on earth can she be going—again—at this time of day, and on a Sunday too?

"What do you think Mother's up to?" I ask Flossie.

"I'm sure that's none of our business, young lady," she replies.

Oh well. Maybe she's visiting another one of her lovey-friends, post nip-and-tuck, at the local private hospital.

I suddenly get a fluttering feeling in my stomach at the thought of seeing Sydney tomorrow at school. I thought I might call him earlier, but then I lost my nerve—although it might have been a good idea as I don't want him to be too overexcited all at once, what with seeing me again for the first time after a whole week. And you know what they say, "Absence makes the heart grow fonder."

I think that instead I'll quickly make a batch of my stupendous heart-shaped bix and wrap them up with the long, newsy, passionate letter I wrote him this morning and then I'll pop the box into his locker as a fantastic surprise.

Flossie tuts a lot while I'm making the bix. She says I'm getting in her way and that thirty-six biscuits for one person is too much. What does she know? And anyway, she always makes Diggory, our gardener, piles of yummies when it's his day on. I just tell her to "shush" as I have to concentrate on pouring passion into the mixture. I read somewhere that if you cook with love it makes the people who are eating your food feel the love too. I want to be sure that Sydney's stomach detects this vital ingredient and that the vital ingredient goes straight to his heart like Mr. Dreamy Dimples said it would.

Upstairs in Heaven while I'm waiting for my cookies to cool I practice my American accent. "Hi, Sydney," I drawl, flicking my hair behind my ear. "How YOU doin'?" *à la* Joey in *Friends*. I get right up close to the mirror and imagine that it's Sydney's eyes I'm gazing into, not mine, while I try out my slow, sexy, scintillating smile. I practice the prepassion pout a bit and just find myself SO devastating, I wonder how Sydney could possibly resist? If I do the pout and the accent *and* the modelly walk that I have perfected over the last few weeks all at once, he won't stand a chance. He'll be swept off his sneakers, fall into

my arms, and we'll have masses of those meringue-flavored kisses before he tells me that his cup runneth over . . . with LURVE. This will make a *very* nice change, as Sydney has been just a little bit of a tease in the past and made not very kind jokes about my cups running over—and we're talking "cups" as in underwear here . . .

I'm contemplating my navel, which is something we do in yoga (although you're not supposed to be thinking about how it needs liposuction) and I hear, above the grungy moans coming from George's boom box that Mother is back. She's shrieking at somebody. I'll see if I can walk to the door to listen while holding my tummy in. I can, but I feel quite faint after a few moments, and as there would be no point in fainting when there is no one to see me, I breathe out again quickly.

Opening the door a crack I can hear that she is in full volcanic eruption. I don't think it's me she's shouting at. No . . . it's Stinker. Come to think of it, Mother hardly ever shouts at me these days. She's so busy wafting about *outside* the house that she barely takes any notice of what I'm up to. Cool!

*ooooops!*

Stinker's eaten one of her Gina slingbacks. Phew! I thought for a moment that he might have demolished something important like my heart-shaped bix.

As soon as Mother has gone to lie down in her darkened room to get over the shock of losing one of her nearest and dearest (and we mean dear in the expensive way here), the coast is clear for me to go downstairs and pack up Sydney's Special Surprise.

I decide not to put the passionate letter in with the biscuits. I think it would be more romantic

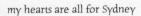
*my hearts are all for Sydney*

for him to find this beautiful tissue-lined box, nestling anony-mously among his locker's innermost secrets. (I hope he hasn't got his smelly gym uniform in there—don't want my little yummy box muddled up with his sweaty socks!)

Crumbs! I don't know the combination for his locker. Oh, panic! How am I going to make my way into Sydney's heart through his stomach if I can't even make my way into his locker? I'll have to call Portia—she'll know what to do.

"Hi, babes!" I say. "Isn't it, like, pretty pukka having Mercedes back?"

"Oh, hi. Yeah, it's great," she says, but she sounds really low.

"Wazzup, babes?" I say, giving my new accent a whirl.

"Nothing really," she sighs. "It's just my mum. We've had a fight. She won't let me invite you guys over after school. She says we'll make a mess and that she's too tired to clean up after us all. She's being really ratty these days."

What is it with mothers at the moment? Portia's mother is usually really sweet. Perhaps there's some weird virus going around that only hits mums and makes them all act peculiar.

"Oh," I say, deciding not to share my virus theory. One of the things I love about Portia's house is that it's always friendly and not terribly tidy (although Portia's room is surgically clean, as she has a bit of a THING about germs—Eau de Disinfectant being her favorite smell). You're never made to feel that you can't sit wherever you'd like. Whereas *here* Mother tuts at me if I so much as *look* at her deep pile velvet living room sofa. She nearly has a breakdown if I dare to place my dainty little bot (not) near one

29

of the cushions. Mind you, now that she's out all the time I can bounce up and down as much as I like on the cushions and by the time she gets home she wouldn't even guess what "bot-attacks" have befallen them.

"Don't worry," I say, trying to sound upbeat. "You can always come around here and no one cares what we do in Heaven. Mother so seldom comes up here that she needs radar tracking just to find it."

"I know," says Portia, "and we all love coming to your house —the food's fantastic—" (Portia eats about three times as much as me, but you could make about three Portias out of my body —life is such a witch) "but I really wanted to be able to ask you back here to sort of say thank-you for all the brilliant times we've had with you and Flossie."

"Well, I tell you what. I've thought of another way you can say thank-you. Find out the combination of Sydney's locker for me. I have to put a little surprise parcel in there for him."

"I don't think that will be too hard," Portia chuckles and I feel pleased that I've managed to cheer her up a bit, but I'm sure I don't know what she's finding funny.

"I'll look over his shoulder for you before homeroom tomor-row. You know how good I am at detective work . . ."

"Thanks, babes," I say. "See you in the morning—and don't worry about your mum. Maybe she's been working too hard or perhaps she needs extra hormones like Mother. *She* gets topped up at least twice a year, but she's still as ratty as a rabid Rottweiler."

"Yeah. Maybe," says Portia. "Bye."

I'm so crazy with excitement about sneaking the biscuits

into Sydney's locker that when George makes his way up to Heaven (to whine some more about his A-levels, no doubt), I tell him about my plan.

He scowls at me and says that he thinks Sydney's a complete saddo and why am I wasting my time and Flossie's ingredients on such a dweeb?

I throw my Nine West pink, kitten-heeled, snakeskin shoe at him (and miss) and tell him never to darken the door of Heaven again. Then I sit down and begin the long wait until tomorrow.

## chapter four

# A Locker Fulla Love

THIS HAS TO be the first time I've ever been pleased to see Mrs. Sophie Something-Hyphenated and her upchuck children. I'm so excited this morning that I almost *kiss* them when they come to collect me to take me to school. I must be crazy with love.

Mrs. Sophie Something-Hyphenated catches my eye in the mirror and gives me one of her "caring" smiles. And I smile back! This being in love thing does have the strangest effects.

"Why are you smiling?" asks Odious Offspring Senior. "I bet you've got a boyfriend." He's looking at me with a disgusting, smarmy smirk that on any other day would make me want to give him a good pinching. I only put up with this humiliating journey to school because Flossie hasn't time to drive me in the morning and if I went by bus I would have to leave home WAY too early for a girl who needs at least half an hour to put on her makeup.

"I might have a boyfriend," I say, trying to look enigmatic and mysterious.

how could anyone love children like these??

little piggy pigtails

often practices farting and burping on the way to school (divine—NOT)

"Have you snogged him?" asks Odious Offspring Junior, peering up at me so closely that I can smell the veggie nut loaf she must have had for supper last night. Either that or she's got something dead in her pocket.

"None of your business," I reply and turn to look wistfully out of the window.

"Did you use tongues? I bet you did!" she whispers, way too close for comfort. I'm about to swat her like the festering flea that she is when we arrive . . . and I am within moments of seeing the L of my L—Sydney.

I jump out and leave the Stinkmobile to drop its loathsome load at the primary school next door.

"Hey! Wait for me!" I squeal to my gorgeous friends as I catch sight of them strolling across the playground. I bound over to them as fast as I can, doing my best to look glam and modelly at the same time.

"Did you get it?" I ask Portia, all breathy with excitement.

"Not yet," she replies, "but Sydney should be going to his locker to collect his stuff for first period any minute now. You wait here. I'll see what I can do," she says and scuttles off in the direction of the lockers.

I wait with Minnie and Mercedes, who, for some incomprehensible reason, has decided to come to school even though she doesn't have to. I mean, she finished her term in America and you would think she would be feeling way too jet-lagged to bother staggering in to school.

But it's just nice to have her here. I hold my breath until Portia scuttles, back looking triumphant.

"You saw him!" I gasp, feeling certain that this is the moment when I am going to faint.

"Yup," says Portia.

I sway around a bit, but I find that my jelly legs haven't collapsed dramatically beneath me after all. "How IS he? Does he look as divine as ever?"

"Yeees . . ." says Portia uncertainly (why?). "Anyway, I got the number for you. It was so easy. He had no idea I was watching his every move."

"He was probably distracted by the thought of seeing me," I say, clasping my hands in front of me in what I think of as my Angelic pose.

"Anyway, here you are," says Portia, handing me a bit of paper with the number written on it. "Do you want us to come with you while you make the drop?"

"It's all right. I'll go alone," I say, secretly hoping that Sydney will have forgotten something and I will bump into him, all unexpectedly, behind the bike sheds on the way to the lockers.

But there is no one around when I pop my labor of love in among his books. I close the locker and secretly seal it with a kiss before skipping lightly off to our classroom for homeroom.

Nobody really notices when I enter. Everyone is milling around Mercedes, which I suppose is understandable, and I can't even see Sydney.

Then, only about a minute later, the door opens and a heavenly choir begins to sing. Sydney enters. The room is flooded with light and I feel my heart swell in my chest ... he's carrying my biccy box. He must have gone back to his locker just after I made the drop ... I only just missed him ... oooooooohhhh!!! How could George call him a saddo? Look at him—he's divine, a god ... I wait for him to come over to me and look lovingly into my eyes and say

twit-face—
wouldn't recognize
a romantic gesture
if it got up and
bit him

lovely, luscious love
of my life with his
BACK to me

**Sydney (back view)**

35

in the softest, gentlest voice, "You truly are an Angel and I adore you."

Fluttering back from my heavenly hallucination I see that Sydney is *not* coming over to talk to me. In fact, I don't even think he's noticed me. Instead he is over in the corner with a huddle of boys and they are all eating my biscuits and laughing.

That can't be right.

I try to rewind to the bit where he comes in through the door, because surely I'm imagining it . . . ? But no . . . SOB. Maybe he's too shy to show me how much he adores me in front of his friends. Obviously, he'll wait until we can be alone together . . .

When class is over and we're heading out of the room, I wait for Sydney's winning smile to light up my life. I stare at the back of his neck and will him to turn around. The back of his neck goes slightly pink as if he knows my eyes are caressing it. But is he the *only* person in the entire room who doesn't seem to notice me???

YES.

Oh no. I can feel tears welling up in my eyes and my nose and my ears feel pink and splotchy. Why won't he look at me?

"Why won't he speak to me or even look at me properly?" I wail when I am finally alone with my best, best friends.

"Don't worry, Angel," says Minnie. "I expect he's too shy to speak to you in front of us all."

"He wasn't too shy to tease me in front of everyone before we were in love. All that stuff he used to do—calling me Jelly Cooking Potts and blabbing on about my cups running over . . . So how come he's too shy today, when he's finally got the chance to tell me how much he cares?"

There's a sort of pause . . .

"Oh! He'll probably write you a note," says Mercedes. It's so nice that she's here. She always says such comforting things. "I expect he's writing it now and you'll, like, find it pushed under the door of your locker after break."

"Maybe he didn't realize that the biscuits were from you," says Portia.

"He must have known they were from me," I sob. "No one else loves him enough to bake him things."

"No, that's true . . ." says Minnie. "But honestly, Angel, you know how Neanderthal boys are. You have to hit them with a wooden club before they notice anything."

I'm sort of comforted by the thought that Sydney is probably writing me a long and loving letter in some dark, private corner of the school when the bell rings for PE. Yuck.

I scamper to my locker to collect my gym uniform and to look for Sydney's note . . .

The trouble is that it takes a long time to write the sort of thing that I know Sydney will want me to read. That must be why his note hasn't made it into my locker yet. He'll probably put it in there after lunch.

I squidge into my sports gear and do my usual dodge down the corridors, hiding behind doors and pillars on the way to the gym to make sure that not one single boy spots me in my TOO-shorts.

Once we're all in there we have to do all sorts of terribly unladylike jogging about. But today I'm wrapped in a soft, pink cloud of anticipation and I hardly notice any of it. When we're

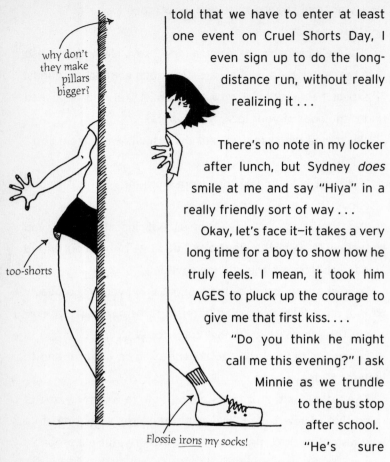

why don't they make pillars bigger?

too-shorts

Flossie irons my socks!

told that we have to enter at least one event on Cruel Shorts Day, I even sign up to do the long-distance run, without really realizing it . . .

There's no note in my locker after lunch, but Sydney *does* smile at me and say "Hiya" in a really friendly sort of way . . .

Okay, let's face it—it takes a very long time for a boy to show how he truly feels. I mean, it took him AGES to pluck up the courage to give me that first kiss. . . .

"Do you think he might call me this evening?" I ask Minnie as we trundle to the bus stop after school.

"He's sure to," she says. "And if not this evening, definitely tomorrow. . . . Maybe he's texted you—have you checked your phone?"

"Fifteen times since lunch and there's still nothing. But he did smile beautifully at me twice—once at lunch and once during science."

"Was that after Mr. Jeffries asked you a question and you answered in that funny accent?" asks Minnie.

"Yes, I suppose it might have been. But then I noticed him

watching me walk across the classroom during English. He looked spellbound . . ."

"Was that when you were doing your modelly walk?" asks Portia.

"Yes," I say. "I think he was properly impressed by that . . . Oh no! What if he tries to phone me while I'm at the gym? He might think that I don't love him any more if I don't answer my phone."

"Don't worry, Angel," says Minnie. "He'll leave a message if you don't answer. Anyway, it's really cool to be unavailable sometimes. You don't want him thinking you're hanging around just waiting for him to call."

"Oh," I say, thinking that I don't really want to risk being unavailable in case Sydney loses interest in the meantime.

Mercedes gives me a hug. "I love you, homegirl," she says. "You'll always, like, have me and the others no matter how many times Sydney gives you highside."

"I know . . ." I say—although I'm not entirely sure I understand what she's talking about.

Things suddenly look brighter as I'm heading to the bus stop. There's Sydney! And HE'S COMING OVER!

He says, "Hi, Angel! Great biscuits!" and then walks a few steps with me toward the bus stop.

My heart is pounding and I can't speak. Why won't any of the words I want to say come out of my mouth? He knew the biscuits were from me! He *does* love me! I know that at any moment he's going to ask me out . . .

But what does he do? He sees some friends on the other side of the road and runs off, calling, "See ya!" to me over his shoulder.

Oh, KNICKERS!

When I get home, I tell Flossie and Potty that I'm off to the gym. Mother's out, as usual. Potty doesn't know where she is ("Too busy looking into this new marmalade Alfie's just discovered. Didn't even notice the old thing wasn't here").

What is keeping Mother so *busy*? Perhaps she's become an artist's model and is posing naked for some famous painter? Or maybe she's gambling away the family fortune. But then surely she wouldn't be looking so happy . . .

"Don't you wonder sometimes what she's up to?" I ask Potty.

"Never gave it a thought, Cherub," he continues. "Anyway, what's afoot?"

I tell him it's the bit at the end of your leg. I just can't bring myself to tell him about Sydney.

# Something Doughy Ma
# Made With Marmalade
*(except Flossie made it)*

| BATTER | TOPPING |
|---|---|
| 1½ cups plain flour | 7½ tbsp marmalade |
| ½ tspn salt | 2½ tbsp powdered sugar |
| 3 eggs | (for dusting) |
| ⅖ cup milk | |
| ⅖ cup water | 5 tbsp cooking oil |
| | (for greasing) |

---

Heat the oven to 400°.

To make the batter, sift the flour and salt into a mixing bowl. Make a little well (dip) in the center of the flour and break the eggs into it. Using an electric whisk, beat the eggs. Gradually beat in the milk, then the water, drawing in the flour from the sides until it is all mixed in and you have a smooth batter.

Put the oil in a 10" x 10" roasting pan and heat it in the oven for about 5 minutes, or until the oil is really hot. (Please be careful when you take the roasting pan out of the oven.) Pour the batter mixture into the roasting pan and bake for 20 to 25 minutes until it has puffed up and is a golden brown color.

Take the cake out of the oven and spread the marmalade over the top. Sift the powdered sugar over the marmalade and pop it back in the oven for a couple of minutes, which will make it beautifully brown and bubbly.

Take the cake out of the oven and cut it into wedges while it's still in the pan. Eat as soon as you can. Even more yummy served with a blob of whipped cream!

## chapter five

# Cruel Shorts and Cupid Cakes

**THE FABBIEST THING** about kickboxing is that you can get rid of all the grotty, grumpy bits that have collected in your head during the day while you do your stances and kick combinations. I imagine I'm getting George in an arm lock for being so rude about Sydney. It's a good thing he's going off on his travels soon. At least it'll stop him from being grotty about my BOYFRIEND . . .

If he *is* my boyfriend, that is.

By the time I get to my yoga class after kickboxing, I'm so in control, even my bottom doesn't dare to wobble. I love yoga. I'm really good at the lying on the floor and visualizing bit.

While I'm lying on the floor, visualizing Sydney and me wandering along a perfect beach in paradise with the waves slooshing and the sun shining, I suddenly have A Very Good Idea.

I'll plan a Cupid Campaign. This will involve food, obviously (Divine Superstar JONC will never desert me, no matter how many times my heart is broken). But I'll also need to be sure

moi, in perfect yogic position, having a Very Good Idea

eat your greens

why doesn't my tummy stay this flat when I stand up?

that the wobble factor is under control, which will mean coming to the gym as much as poss, so as not to make a twit of myself at Cruel Shorts Day.

I have to get Sydney to admit his adoration for me before we go to Italy. That way I can be sure that he will wait, lovesick and lonely, until I come home to his strong and loving arms.

I have a very short time to reach my goal. This calls for immediate action!

I go straight home from the gym, full of vim and vigor or something . . . anyway, feeling terribly organized. When George asks me why I'm looking so cheerful, I tell him it's because he's going away soon and that I have made Important Decisions.

"Which are . . . ?" he asks, doing that Pierce Brosnan raised-eyebrow thing.

"Which are," I reply, "absolutely none of your business. Now leave me," I say with a dramatic wave of my hand. "I have things to attend to."

He grumbles off, mumbling something under his breath, but loud enough for me to hear about Sydney being a saddo.

I do a little yogic breathing to wipe George from my mind and concentrate on more important matters.

# THE CUPID CAMPAIGN

### Number One:
### Impress Sydney on Cruel Shorts Day

Go to the gym as often as possible.

Practice running a bit.

Don't really "do" running.

Don't really like running.

Boobs bounce dangerously close to chin.

Will either end up in casualty department of local hospital or lingerie department of local store.

I decide that the lingerie department in Harrods (just a hop, skip, and a jump away) is a safer bet and buy a sports bra, using Mother's charge account, then I try running again.

**Result:** Running is still horrible, but much less danger-ous. Will know result on Cruel Shorts Day.

### Number Two: Angel Food Cake

This will be the first scrumptious little something that I make for Sydney in the Cupid Campaign. Using Mercedes's tin, I produce the gorgeous, light dreamy number. I pack it into a round, pink plastic box and place it tenderly on Sydney's backpack, which I find lying on the floor in our classroom during break the next day.

**Result:** Zilch, nuffink, nil, zero.

No smile, no "thank you", no "I love you," no kiss, not even a look in my direction . . . but a sort of swoop of beastly boys who cram big wodges of the dreamy stuff into their cake holes before the next lesson begins.

Mercedes tells me that perhaps I should "chill" and wait for Sydney to make the next move.

BUM.

### Number Three: Fascinating letter-making assignation

I place the letter in Sydney's locker (luckily having taken a deep breath before opening the door, as this time his gym uinform is in there—gosh, you have to love a man an awful lot to live with socks like those).

Feel sure that Sydney will turn up at the appointed time and place.

**Result:** He doesn't turn up.

Instead, I come across him lurking behind the science lab door as I walk past. "Hi!" I say in my most breezy

and breathtakingly beautiful way. I pucker up a bit for a smacking kiss and what does he do?

Runs away as if I had something contagious.

Portia says that I must be careful not to make a fool of myself and that it's undignified to chase after a boy.

PANTS.

Will dollop strawberry-flavored Angel Delight instant pudding into his sneakers if he doesn't speak to me soon.

## Number Four: Ask girlies' advice

**Result:** Minnie says, "Definitely cool it," and "When do George and Jimmie go off to the West Indies?" and, "How long did you say they were going to be away?"

Mercedes says, "It could just be that Sydney isn't worth it. I think you should cool it. He's not good enough for you."

Portia says, "He must be a twit if he can't see how gorgeous you are," and says, "cool it" and that she is really worried about her mum, who is tired and crotchety all the time and looks like death warmed up.

Will try to be more understanding and caring when Cupid Campaign is concluded.

## Number Five: Ask Mother and Potty's advice

I would do this, but: (a) Potty is too old to understand and anyway he is yomping his way through a yogurt mountain, having just completed his Marmite campaign, and (b) I was kind of joking about asking Mother and besides, she is almost never at home and when she is, she is always on the phone. I heard her talking to someone called Filippo and telling him that she would see him at three tomorrow, as usual.

Haven't a clue who Filippo is. Would investigate this if wasn't so busy with Cupid Campaign.

**Result:** Failure.

## Number Six: Ask Flossie's advice

**Result:** She says that boys like a bit of mystery (i.e., cool it). She also says that she has only seen Mother once or twice in the last few days, but that it's nice that she is taking an interest in something.

The Cupid Campaign is not really going according to plan.

It's already the morning of Cruel Shorts Day and I've still hardly even succeeded in getting Sydney to talk to me. George and Jimmie left yesterday for the West Indies, but not before George said that anyone who doesn't even bother to say thank-you for all the nosh I've made him over the past couple of weeks ought to be strung up by his ears. I can't help but think he may have a point.

"He's got to show me that he loves me before we go to Italy," I whine to Minnie, "otherwise I may never be happy again."

"Maybe you should try to think of all those Italian stallions instead," Minnie giggles.

"Must I?" I sigh, in a sort of world-weary way. "Italian stallions are so not my thing. Sydney Arthur David Mann is the only one I shall ever love. I know he loves me—he just needs a little urging."

"Perhaps that should be 'purging'," says Minnie, "to get him moving."

She's giggling again, but really, this is no laughing matter. Term finishes tomorrow and then we only have three days to get ourselves together before we leave for Italy.

It's a boiling hot day and Portia and Mercedes are looking amazing in their shorts. As Minnie is swimming, she won't be wearing her cruel shorts today. I am supposed to be wearing mine, but I have been putting it off.

49

I suddenly get seriously panicky at the thought of letting my poor, splotchy, winter-white, oh-so-slightly wobbly legs see the light of day and the glare of the spectators. Luckily none of my family is here to embarrass me. Mother doesn't understand the concept of Sports Day—shopping at the sales is the closest she's ever come to any sport (anyway, she says that any jumping up and down makes the facial muscles droop)—and Potty is tasting cheeses with Alfie. This is a very good thing, as the last time he came to Sports Day he arrived in his sports jacket and pajama trousers, carrying his old wood-framed tennis racquet. He kept shouting, "Jolly hockey sticks!" during the races and telling people that it "simply wasn't cricket."

I'm so totally panicky now at the thought of Sydney seeing me in my cruel shorts that I decide to wear my sweatpants instead. Not elegant, it has to be said, but very mysterious, so I expect that Flossie would approve.

My race is almost the last, which means I get to watch everyone else go first. This is so not fun. My tummy keeps sort of lurching around like a rubber duck in a bathtub and I'm getting hotter and hotter in my navy fleece.

But panic turns to passion when Sydney does his races. He's so sporty and FIT—in both senses of the word. He does incredibly well and I scream myself hoarse as he pounds around the track. I'm sooo proud of him and I would so love to give him a great big kiss . . .

When it's my turn, I line up on the track and look around at all the other competitors. Crumbs! Don't all these people look sporty? I think to myself that I'm never going to be able to do this—I've never managed to finish a whole race in my life. I'm so hot already and I've only walked to the starting line so far. I try to do some yogic breathing to calm my nerves. Then I look up and around the stadium to see if I can see the girlies and yes, there they are waving and smiling from the finish line, but who's that standing a couple of feet away from them . . . is that Sydney?

AAARGH! I'm hotter than ever now and BANG! We're off . . .

I pound steadily along the track, chanting, "Don't wobble, no trouble, don't wobble, no trouble," to myself under my breath. I feel a bit cooler with the wind rushing past me . . . and it really is . . . I am actually doing it . . . I'M RUNNING!

I'm so hot you could fry eggs on my face

inside these sweat-pants are legs that ran a WHOLE RACE —impressive or what?

I've done four laps . . . five . . . six . . . only two more to go and my bra straps haven't bust (HA!) so I haven't fallen over my boobs or anything yet . . .

All of a sudden there's a cheer and I know that someone has won. It isn't me, but it's someone not too far ahead and if I *really* try I might . . . get . . . there . . .

I DID IT!! I finished the long-distance run for the first time in my entire life. I RAN! I'm out of breath, but I prance about anyway, feeling sporty and snazzy in my unbearably hot sweatpants. I DID IT! Hee, hee! I'm a star. I didn't knock myself out with my boobs, I didn't collapse in a heap and cry like one or two of the other poor people competing today. I, Angelica Cookson Potts, ran a race and FINISHED IT!

The girlies come over to congratulate me, but where is Sydney? He must be so impressed that surely he will rush to my side to see if I need mouth-to-mouth resuscitation (and I might, easily—I'm so hot now that a well-cooked lobster would look icy next to me). I think I'd better faint. That'll bring him running. I put my head in my hands and reel around a little.

"What's the matter, Angel?" asks Mercedes. "Are you sick?"

"Yes," I moan. "I'm sick . . ." I peek through my fingers to see if I can see Sydney. And what does he do? WALK AWAY!

"I'm sick," I screech in a last-ditch attempt to make him turn around, and then, much more quietly, I groan to my friends, "I'M TOTALLY SICK OF SYDNEY NOT NOTICING ME."

# Cupid's Own Angel Cake

WARNING: you will need LOTS of eggs for this recipe, so either befriend a chicken or stock up at the supermarket.

*1 cup plain flour, sifted*
*1½ cups sugar*
*1 cup egg whites (you will probably need 8 or 9 eggs for this—use the yolks to make scrumptious scrambled eggs)*

*½ tsp salt*
*1 tsp cream of tartar*
*½ tsp vanilla extract*
*½ tsp of almond extract*

———

Heat the oven to 375°.

Sift the flour with half a cup of the sugar into a bowl and put to one side. In another, larger bowl, using an electric whisk, beat the egg whites with the salt until they are frothy. Sift the cream of tartar into the egg whites and beat until they will stand up in little peaks when you lift out the beaters. Sprinkle 4 tablespoons of the remaining sugar over the egg whites and beat thoroughly. Add the rest of the sugar, 4 tablespoons at a time, beating thoroughly after each addition. Beat in the vanilla and almond extract.

Sift a little of the flour and sugar mixture you prepared at the beginning over the egg mixture and fold it in carefully after each addition. ("Folding in" means gently mixing with a metal spoon, lifting the mixture as you do so to let in air. You mustn't use a wooden spoon or all the froth will disappear from the egg mixture and it will go all yucky.)

Spoon the mixture into a wonderful Angel Food Cake pan, which looks sort of like a tube, and bake it in the preheated oven for 35 to 45 minutes. Test that the cake is cooked by touching it lightly with your fingertip. If it is cooked it will spring back.

Remove the cake from the oven. Invert the cake pan and leave to cool for about 2 hours. When it's cool run a knife around the inside edge of the pan and ease the cake out.

chapter six

# Thing Me a Thong

"MY MUM IS looking completely wiped-out these days," Portia tells us while we're lolling around in Heaven. "Although she says she's fine, I'm kind of worried about leaving her. I wish she would tell me what's the matter. I'm sort of scared that something awful is going to happen. But she says it's good that I'm going to have a holiday and I am really happy to be going." Then, looking over at me in my misery, "Come on, Angel. You must try and cheer up. Much worse things happen to people all the time. And anyway, term's over now which is great and that tea Ms. Worhause laid gave us after Sports Day was fantastic. You really enjoyed yourself, didn't you?"

"S'pose so," I say gloomily.

"And aren't you happy for me?" says Mercedes in her old un-American English. "I'm so lucky Paul has asked me to go out with him when we get back from Italy. I really thought that he might dump me while I was away in America . . . It does seem awful to be leaving him again so soon, but, hey–

he says he won't mind waiting, and I'm really excited about going on holiday with you babes."

"I'm so glad your grandparents agreed to let you come . . . Have you loved Paul all this time?" I ask between sniffles. Actually, I can't believe I haven't talked to Mercedes about Paul since she's been back—I've been so wound up in my own Sydney saga that I've kind of ignored everyone else's love life. But it does cheer me up a little to think that there are *some* nice boys in our class and that one of them knows how to treat a girl.

"Yes," Mercedes answers coyly, "I've loved him ever since the Valentine disco. He wrote to me all the time when I was in Florida. I just couldn't think of dating anyone else."

"Ahhhh . . ." the rest of us say in unison. "You never said."

There's a pause while we all look dreamily into the distance —until I remember that my heart is breaking and I may never recover.

"I can't leave Sydney without something to remember me by. He may not exactly realize it now, but in time I'm sure he will see that I am the one."

Minnie sighs loudly and Portia very gently says that Sydney may not be quite the person I would like him to be. I don't want to think about this possibility and think instead about what little thing I could give him. I'm considering giving him a signed photograph, when I suddenly have another Very Good Idea.

"I know," I say, all excited by my own brilliance, "I'll give Sydney a year's supply of Love Hearts—that way he'll be able to have something sweet every day to remember me by. Come on—let's go straight to Harrods now and buy up their entire stock."

"Does Harrods sell Love Hearts?" asks Portia anxiously.

"Of course they do!" I whoop as I dash around the room, collecting the essentials for a Love Heart shopping spree. "You could buy an elephant there if you wanted to!"

"Let's not buy an elephant," says Mercedes, looking all crumpled with worry. "That would be so cruel. I'm sure elephants don't belong in Knightsbridge."

"Don't be a goof," I say, giving her a hug. "We're going to buy edibles not animals. Now come on, let's go!"

"Shall we look at bikinis as well while we're there?" asks Minnie. "Or perhaps we could look at bikinis *instead*."

"Spectacular plan, but there is no way we are going to look at swimwear without getting something for Sydney," I say, without really thinking about what bikini buying means, so thrilled am I with my sweetie treatie idea for Sydney.

We hurtle down the stairs and run into Mother, who's coming back in. She's looking what *Vogue* calls "radiant." She hasn't done her rabid Rottweiler act for ages. She also hasn't got any parcels with her. This is so unusual that I have to look very hard at her

this is the hand that usually holds the parcels

to make sure that this really is my mother. It is.

"Hi!" I say. "Where have you been?"

"Oh, here and there," she says, almost smiling, but without crinkling her eyes too much.

"Where and where?" I ask again, feeling bold since coming up with my Brilliant Idea.

"*Cattiva ragazza!* That, dahling, is for me to know and you to stop asking."

"Oh . . ." I say as Mother shrugs off her Dior jacket and glides, humming a little Mozart, into the living room.

Spooky! I have the urge to stay and tie Mother to a chair, shine a bright light in her eyes and question her closely as to where it is she keeps going, *à la* James Bond . . .

No, I don't really mean it about the chair and the tying and the light, but I would like to know what's going on . . .

The others are jostling me. "Come on, Angel," squeaks Minnie. "We're on a mission."

"A Mission of Passion," giggles Mercedes—then, suddenly looking serious, she says, "Angel, are you sure about this?"

"Course I am," I say. "Come on!" And we swing out of the door and into the balmy warmth of the Knightsbridge car fumes.

Mother calls out from the living room window, "Dahlings! Buy yourselves some really good sunscreens if you're going to Harrods. A girl is never safe abroad without at least Factor 20 on any part of her that is to see the slightest sparkle of sunlight. Remember . . ."

"Mr. Sunlight is Mrs. Wrinkle's best friend . . ." all four of us trill in unison.

"Put it on my account, dahling, and be sure to get the best."

"Okay," I yell back, thinking that Mother really is being very peculiar and, quite honestly, I'm not sure I really like this . . . I mean, has she actually changed or has she been hit on the head?

While we're strutting our stuff to Harrods (just a catwalk strip away), I ask the girls whether they think Mother is acting strangely.

"She's not nearly as odd as my mum is at the moment," sighs Portia. I put my arm around her and give her a reassuring little squeeze.

never mind, Charlie, these are Angel's angels

Mother gave me this for Christmas— it's got a picture of *moi* on it

obviously there are no talent scouts around today or we would all be snapped up IMMEDIATELY

"Try not to worry," says Mercedes. "Honestly, I'm sure she would tell you if there was something really wrong."

"Angel, I don't think your mother's being strange at all," says Minnie, turning to face me. "She just looks really happy, as if there is something wonderful happening in her life—perhaps she's having an affair!" And the three of them double over with giggles.

"Minnie!" cries Mercedes. "That's an awful thing to say. Angel's mother is much too old to be doing . . . Oh! Sorry, Angel. I didn't mean it like that—I just meant that she was too, you know, grown-up to do anything so silly and she would *never* do that to Potty."

I'm laughing away with the others when we reach the doors of Harrods. We quickly locate the sweetie department and I find out that I have to order the Love Hearts, but they say they will be able to get them in and deliver them by courier to Sydney's home tomorrow. I only saw him yesterday at Sports Day, but I'm missing him so much already. I make the smiley lady behind the counter promise to have the Love Hearts all packed up beautifully. I ask her to enclose a little card with a chubby cupid on it, that I find in the stationery department and on which I write:

*If you're feeling strangel*
*Without your Angel*
*And skies are gray*
*While I'm away,*
*Don't be blue*
*'Cos I'm thinking of YOU.*

I'm not terribly pleased with the poem, but it's hard to think of something stupendous when all your friends are looking over your shoulder and making silly suggestions or telling you that you shouldn't be sending your boyfriend anything at all.

"Now can we go and look at bikinis?" asks Minnie.

So we troop off to the swimwear department, but not before I realize that the only thing I've waxed in the last few months is a bit of my bedside table when one of my scented candles fell over.

"Babes?" I say uncertainly. "Do you really think this is a good idea?"

"Of course it is," says Portia. "We're here, the bikinis are here, and we're going to Italy in two days' time! And anyway, you said it was a stupendous idea before, so what's different now?"

"I've just remembered I've got gorilla legs," I whisper.

"No, you haven't," says Minnie. "Your legs looked fine on Sports Day."

"That's because I was wearing my sweatpants," I reply. "And anyway," I add, lowering my voice, as there are lots of people around, "my legs aren't the only hairy bits that, you know, *need doing*."

"Well, don't worry," Minnie whispers back. "You can stay in your changing room and no one but you need see your hairy bits."

"Promise you won't peek?"

They all promise not to so much as knock at my changing-room door without giving me at least a two-minute warning.

The others start looking at titchy-witchy-eeeny-weeny-brightly-colored-posh bikinis and I shuffle over to the one-pieces with extra support and built-in scaffolding. Perhaps one of these with the skirt affair that is meant to skim those thighs and to kindly take the eye away from any problem areas would do?

I trawl through the Lycra lovelies that look big enough to house a hippopotamus. Maybe black? Maybe black with a high neck and cycling-type shorts with a skirt thing over the top? And then a huge T-shirt to finish the ensemble?

"I don't want everyone to stare at me on the beach," I say to the others as they ask what on earth I'm doing.

"Well, they'll definitely stare at you if you dare to wear one of these monstrosities," says Portia. "Come and look at the bikinis. They are way more flattering than these great big things . . . have you made a list of the things you are going to take with you so that we can color coordinate?"

I am about to laugh, but then I see that Portia is deadly serious and has brought her own list of Things to Take on Holiday. "No," I say, "but I had thought black would be a good bet."

"No, no, no," says Minnie, who knows about fashion things. "You must wear a wonderful, bright, zingy color that will glow in the sunshine and show off the tan you're going to get."

"Do I want to zing and glow?" I ask, thinking that "zing and glow" sounds like things a microwave oven might do.

"Of *course* you do," she says before scampering off and returning with three hangers, full of fun. "There you are! Try these on."

GULP.

We head to the changing rooms.

CRIKEY.

"This one's got no bottom!" I squeal.

"Whatchya mean?" asks Mercedes from next door while Portia starts singing "The Girl From Ipanima" in the next cubicle.

"It's only got this little tiny thong thing—I can't wear this . . . who is that singing?"

"It's me!" sings Portia. "Sing a thong—you know what they say, 'It's the singer not the song'!"

"Shouldn't that be 'It's the swimmer not the thong?'" I giggle as I pull the bottom half of the bikini on over my sensible knickers.

"AAAARGH!!" I scream. "I can't wear these. I can't even walk properly—I'll look like Hop a'Thong Cassidy if you make me buy this one!"

By this time we're all completely hopeless, gagging with giggles and snorting with laughter. That is, until Mercedes emerges from her cubicle and says, "What do you think?" I stick my head out from behind the door of my cubicle and nearly fall into a dead faint. She looks SENSATIONAL—all coffee-colored gleaming skin with not a dimple to be seen nor a cell of cellulite anywhere, wearing the most blinding bikini that looks as if it's been sprayed on to her. There isn't a curve out of place.

"GOSH!" I say, as it's the only thing I can think of. "That looks just so . . . so . . . YOU. You have to buy it."

Minnie and Portia have tried on everything in their sizes, but neither of them can afford the huge prices (the smaller the swimwear the bigger the cost) and they both have things at

63

home that they think will do. Also, Jimmie has already gone off on his travels with George, and I think Minnie feels that there isn't any point shelling out huge amounts of cash on swimwear that Jimmie won't see.

Mercedes and Minnie become my personal shoppers and Portia is advisor. Between them, my dream team come up with not one, but two fabby-dabby-beach-babe bikinis that really do the business. (Not that I can show the others on account of the fuzzy wuzzies.) They are identical, but in different colors, one black (my choice) and one a zingy pingy pink that Minnie says will look good with my dark hair (I hope she means the hair on my head and not you-know-where). The tops must be brilliantly engineered because they make my boobs look quite neat, and emphasize my cleavage. I don't want to be smug, but do any of my perfect friends have a proper cleavage? No, they don't. (They do have flat stomachs and a total lack of wobblability, but hey ho, you can't have everything.) The bottoms are a kind of semi-thong—not so teensy on the in-betweeny bit that they are in danger of disappearing you-know-where, but not so huge that they look like a pair of Flossie's thermals. If I really pull in my stomach and half close my eyes, I look almost all right.

my not-so-itsy-bitsy-teeny-weeny bikini, in eye-ache pink

I am hungry with happiness.

"Fantabamazing, babes," I say. "Thank you all SO much. I feel nearly ready to rumba now!"

We trot triumphantly back down to the cosmetics department, Mercedes and I both clutching our green and gold bags, and begin the search for the perfect sunscreen, as directed by Mother.

# Love Cuff

This is not so much a recipe as an idea, really.

If you were incredibly clever with your needle (like Minnie) you could make little holes in some Love Hearts and thread them onto a piece of thin elastic, then tie the ends together to make them into a bracelet.

Then you could wear your heart on your sleeve (HA HA!).

# chapter seven

# Love Hearts—Love Hurts

**"HEAVENS TO BETSY,"** says Flossie when I show her my amazing beachwear two days before we leave for Italy. "You'll catch your death in that! You'll get a chill on your kidneys with so little to cover you up—down there."

Flossie is in the kitchen slicing veggies to make a delicious, cold, summer soup. I thought she might be excited about my beautiful bikinis, but actually she's being a bit poo about the whole holiday thing.

Alfie's villa does have its own staff, but Potty wanted Flossie to come with us as she knows all "his little ways." But Flossie doesn't really want to come. She says she doesn't get on with "abroad" and doesn't know how she's going to do the food shopping when the only Italian word she knows is "macaroni." Also, she's not at all thrilled with the idea of having to share a kitchen with "some ITALIAN person."

Deep down, I don't think she wants to leave Diggory to his own devices while we are away. We all know she's got the hots for him, but she's very coy about discussing her relationship with "her little bit of excitement" (as she describes Diggory). She's made him three Dundee cakes and fourteen individual custard tarts for the two weeks that we won't be here . . . and he only comes to do the garden twice a week!

"Are you going to buy a bathing suit, Flossie?" asks Portia. The others have already gone home, but she has decided that she would rather stay here as long as possible because her mum is being so dreary.

"Certainly not," snaps Flossie, but then, seeing that Portia looks a bit upset, she says, "I've got a perfectly good Marks and Spencer all-in-one that I bought in 1962. It's hardly had any wear. Besides I don't expect *I'll* have time to loll around on the beach."

"You could loll by the pool," I say helpfully.

Flossie just "humphs" and says that she "doesn't hold with too much idleness—the devil makes work for idle hands." Portia and I just nod, trying not to giggle.

"I mean, look at this," says Flossie, waving a postcard. "This arrived today from young George. He says that he and Jimmie do nothing all day but go to the beach and 'smirkle.'"

"I think it says 'snorkle,'" I say, taking the postcard from her.

"Well, whatever it is he's doing, it sounds very unsuitable to me . . ."

It's no good trying to talk to Flossie when she's in one of her "moods," so I switch off from the conversation and start to read George's postcard. He says "Hi" to me and Stinker, which is nice, but at the bottom he's written, "Tell Angel to get over Saddo, soonest." Honestly, I think I preferred George when he

was strong and silent and kept his
opinions to himself. I fling the
postcard down on the kitchen
table and say, "Come on, Portia,
let's go and have a beauty session up
in Heaven." I scoop up my shopping
and several homemade cheese
scones—I'm still hungry with happiness after my swimwear success.

postcard
from
George

On the way up to Heaven, we
pass Potty's study and hear him
practicing his Italian. He's got a
teach-yourself-Italian tape, which
says things he has to repeat. Ever
since he finished his extensive research
into the world of blue-veined cheeses,
he's been spending all his time on this.

Flossie
always puts
her hand on
her hip when
she's in a snit

"*Buona sera*," says the tape.

"Bunny Sarah," says Potty.

"*Come stai?*" says the tape.

"Come and stay?" says Potty.

"Hi, Potty," I yell as we pass.

"Helloo," he shouts over the tape. "Howo areo youo? I
speako Italiano nowo!"

It must be brilliant to have normal parents. Potty is just *not
like* anyone else—it can be very embarrassing introducing him
to new people. But I still love him to pieces. I can tell him all
sorts of things, and however odd his advice is, it's usually
worth listening to. He's always really comforting and he never

comments on my size or makes me feel stupid.

Mother, on the other hand, is really good at meeting people, but she hasn't got a clue about Motherliness. Sometimes she looks quite surprised to see me here, as if she had forgotten that she had a daughter at all. I think she'd like me to be decorative, but that's all. I know she loves me in her own way, but I don't think she can be bothered with the sort of messy growing-up issues that my friends and I go through.

I shout "Goodo!" back to Potty, as Portia and I bound over the sleeping Stinker and up the stairs.

Upstairs in the bathroom, Portia chats to me while I wax my legs. "Do you have any wraps?" she asks.

Natch I think she is talking about food so I go on for a while about Parma ham and avocado.

"No, no!" says Portia. "I mean things to cover up with while you're on the beach. You might want to go to a beach bar or stroll along the water's edge without exposing too much."

"Oh yes," I say. "I think I've got something somewhere." But quite honestly I can't keep my mind on this holiday at all. All I can think about is what Sydney will do when he gets all those Love Hearts. He'll be amazed. He'll be overwhelmed. He'll be internally grateful! He'll think I'm the sweetest thing since Doris Day.

He'll come around with an armful of flowers and go down on his knees and BEG me not to leave him, not even for a minute. Then will come the hard part. I shall have to say, "Sydney, my darling, this is as difficult for me as it is for you . . . But I must leave these sceptered isles and go with the tide (Monarch

in a few short
moments this
body will be
tan-tastic!

Airlines, actually) to places far away. But fear not, I shall
return. And then, my darling, we will be reunited, and the
flower of our all-consuming passion will bloom again and we
will never, ever be parted." Fade out to long shot of sunset and
a thousand violins playing in the background . . .

At least I hope that's what will happen. Suddenly I feel my
stomach lurch at the thought that Sydney might not love me
after all . . .

Portia pulls me out of these scary thoughts by suggesting
that we get on with the instant tanning. After we've sloshed on

the Costa-del-Mucho-golden-delicious-beach-babe-super-tan cream, we stand around, eating cheese scones and discussing other people's love lives, while we wait for the glorious glow to develop. We've just got to a really juicy bit about Scarlet the Harlot, the class drama queen, when Portia begins to giggle.

"What is it?" I say, giggling too, because you can't help it when someone else starts.

Portia is doing a proper belly laugh now (except that she hasn't any belly) and my knees are shaking, I'm laughing so much.

"What IS it?" I squeal, and then Portia moves around and the sunlight through the window isn't behind her any more, and I can see her clearly . . .

"YIKES! What's happened to us?" I yell. "How can you laugh? We look like orange humbugs!"

PANIC! I can't lie on a beach looking like this. It's going to be bad enough showing off my bountiful body, next to my perfect friends, without it having tiger stripes as well. And besides, this orange color is going to clash horribly with my pink bikini.

There's only one person who will know what to do. Holding my bath towel tight around me, I rush downstairs, shouting, "Mother, Mother, HELP!"

Potty rushes out of his study. "What's up, little Cherub, has Stinker disgraced himself again? Oh, I say, how jolly. Are we playing cowboys and Indians? Is that your warpaint?"

"No," I wail. "I need Mother. Where is she?"

Potty shouts "Clarissaaaa" for a while, before he remembers that Mother went out a couple of hours ago.

"Oh!" I wail again. "Why is she never here?"

Potty retreats back into his study and I storm back upstairs to Portia. "What are we going to do now? There's no point calling Mercedes—she won't know what to do. She never has to go through this sort of ordeal. She's already that heavenly baked-cookie color. We'll have to call Minnie. Maybe she'll know what to do."

Oh!

We call Minnie, and she spends ages giggling before she can say anything sensible. Finally, she suggests that we both have really hot showers, and use those friction mitt things that Mother is so keen on. "And when you've done that," she says, all prim and proper, "look at the instructions again and see what you did wrong."

"All right," I say. "I'll let you know how it goes."

After what seems like hours of scrubbing and buffing, the worst of the stripes have disappeared and we are both peeled-prawn color and EXHAUSTED. Of course, Minnie is right: we did the whole thing wrong. But reading instructions is so SENSIBLE, isn't it?

To recover, we tuck into plenty of Flossie's soup and freshly baked bread. Then Portia's mum calls, sounding very worried, so Portia decides it's time to go home.

I get my suitcase out and think about packing.

I decide that it doesn't matter what clothes I take on holiday with me since HE won't see me, and I spend the rest of the evening staring at my empty case and waiting for HIM to call.

he would do anything to stop me from leaving him . . .

wish he'd brought me roses—I don't actually like carnations that much

**my fantasy**

Finally I go to bed. But I can't sleep. I spend all night waiting.

And all the next day.

Even when I check with Horrids to make sure that the Love Hearts have been delivered to Sydney, and they have, HE STILL DOESN'T CALL!!

Okay. Playing hard to get, is he? I'll call him. I call him . . . I call him eighteen times and HE DOESN'T PICK UP.

I decide to text him: SWEETHEART U R MY LOVE HEART XXX. But before I send the message I think that perhaps it would be cooler *not* to send it . . . maybe it looks a bit desperate.

Honestly, what is his PROBLEM? Couldn't he even be *polite* and admit that I exist? Or is he too much of a wimp to face me?

POO, BUM, BOTTOM, PANTS, SOB.

I don't care about the holiday any more. I just fling a few old things into my suitcase along with my bikinis. (Which looked a-jolly-mazing when I tried them on again in the middle of the long, lonely night.) What does any of it matter when my heart is in fragments? I shall spend my whole holiday visiting nunneries, with a view to joining one as soon as possible.

## chapter eight

# Flying Flossie

**HOW CAN MOTHER** possibly need so much luggage? I wonder gloomily as I watch the ever-increasing pile in the hallway. We're just about to leave. I've only got my backpack. I won't need much in the nunnery; the nuns will give me one of those nice gray dress things—what are they called? "Habits," I think —and that will cover everything up. Wish I hadn't bothered with the leg wax and fake tan; it'll all be wasted on Mother Superior.

"Stop dawdling," says Flossie. "I'm sure there's something useful you could be doing."

"I could throw myself under the Number Eighteen bus," I say helpfully.

"Angelica Cookson Potts, you're to stop all this nonsense at once," she snaps. "Life isn't always a bowl of cherries. Think about someone other than yourself for a while."

"Oh yes, OF COURSE, OKAY," I snarl. "I'll think about Sydney and how he's broken my heart into a thousand pieces . . ." Or, I think to myself, I could think about J. Oliver Superstar and Naked Chef Extraordinaire—I bet HE would never smash my heart like this . . . He would have appreciated all the yummy nummies I cooked for him . . .

Flossie tuts at me a lot more. She's mega-ratty about this whole holiday thing. She keeps muttering on about "abroad" not being her "favorite place." Finally, she stomps off and fetches her basket of provisions from the kitchen. She's packed all sorts of things that she says "abroad" won't have. There's Marmite, English mustard and Gentlemen's Relish, a plastic box full of shortbread, and one of her homemade fruit-cakes in a flowery tin.

Stinker is sitting in the hallway watching all the fuss. He isn't coming to Italy with us. Mrs. Sophie Something-Hyphenated is looking after him.

Strange things have happened between Mrs. Sophie Something-Hyphenated and Stinker over the past few weeks. Mrs. S S-H adores animals of all kinds and is always campaigning for animal rights, but Stinker used to be the only fluffy creature that she would cheerfully have suffocated. Although a while ago he did something that Changed Her Mind. Someone tried to break into the Stinkmobile, but Stinker was watching from the hall window and he barked so furiously that Mrs. S S-H heard him and rushed out into the street. She arrived on the scene just in time to see the thief beating a hasty retreat, with Stinker still growling and yapping at him through the window. She now thinks that Stinker is "too sweet for words" and has offered to look after him while we are away.

Potty doesn't want to be parted from Stinker for a minute longer than is absolutely necessary, so Mrs. Sophie

stripes this way are so not flattering

biodegradable, recycled, organically farmed cotton— secondhand

Stinker can be such a creep sometimes

Something-Hyphenated is taking us, and Stinker, to the airport in her rancid Range Rover so that Potty won't need to say "good-bye" to him until the last moment.

Potty wobbles out of the house. He looks unusually fat. When he sees me staring at him he says, "Thought I'd wear most of my clothes for the trip, little Cherub. Saves tremendously on the packing. I've even got the old swimmers on under here. Brilliant idea, don't you think?"

I'm too miserable to think about how completely embarrassing my parents are.

Mother is wafting about with a stupid grin on her face. How can anyone look happy when the sky is as gray as Ozzy Osbourne's roots, and my life is so over?

I start to think that perhaps Mother is ill. It could account for her strange change of personality. Maybe she's got some terrible brain disease? That would be just so dreadful . . . I did ask Flossie the other day if she thought Mother might be going slightly mad. But Flossie just told me to respect my elders and not go spreading silly ideas. But I don't know, there is definitely something seriously odd about Mother these days.

"Come on, dahling," she shouts, bringing me back from my musings. She's sitting in the front seat of the Stinkmobile, where she has plonked herself while the rest of us scurry around piling in the luggage. "We're off to *bella Italia*, what could be more fabuloso than that?" The bluebird of happiness is certainly sitting on her shoulder this morning, while the duck of despair is sitting on mine.

"What could be more 'fabuloso' than that," I reply, "is one of you noticing that my life is in ruins. You should all take a long, loving look at me, as I shall be entering an Italian nunnery as soon as I can find one."

"Oh, little Cherub," says Potty, patting my hand. "Somehow I don't see you as a nun; I've heard that sometimes they get very dirty habits! Ha ha! Do you get it, Angel? Nuns, habits? Ha ha!" Everyone thinks this is pants-wettingly funny. Everyone except me, that is.

"Shush, Potty," says Mother. "First love can be a very painful experience. . . . I remember being brokenhearted over MY first boyfriend . . ."

It's all very well, Mother yattering on about her BOYFRIEND, but it's not as if Sydney is really my BOYFRIEND, is it? I mean, if he was my BOYFRIEND he would have taken me out at least once, wouldn't he? I scowl darkly, while Potty organizes the luggage and the adults carry on their conversation as if I wasn't there. Flossie says, "Pay no attention to Angel. She's in a MOOD."

Huh! I like that—when it's Flossie who's been so grumpy about this whole holiday thing.

I humph a bit while the rest of us pile into the Stinkmobile and we set off. As she drives, Mrs. Sophie Something-Hyphenated croaks on and on about her latest recycling adventures. Apparently she's discovered that she can use her old tights to strain her homemade nettle wine through. Yuck—alcoholic athlete's foot! I can see that even Mother, with her newfound *joie de vivre*, is looking a bit nonplussed by that idea. Still, it's taken my mind off BOYFRIENDS—or rather, the *lack* of them—for a while.

We're meeting the others at the airport. We arrive, a bit late, partly because it took Potty so long to say good-bye to Stinker, and partly because Mrs. S S-H had to follow the "scenic route" so that we could all "enjoy the wild grasses along the hedgerows" (along with the empty McDonald's boxes and french fry packets). The girlies have already checked in their luggage.

Portia has made us all labels. There's one for each bit of luggage (she very cleverly figured out that Mother might need more than the rest of us and made extra labels for her) and one for each of us to wear.

"You're supposed to stick them on to your fronts so that we can find each other in a crowd. That way we won't get separated," she explains.

My label is pink with "Angel" written on it. I try very hard to imagine how this will stop me from getting separated from the others. Everyone knows my name is Angel and, anyway, if you can't see a person's face, how are you supposed to see a tiny label? But Portia is so happy with her idea that I think it would be mean to point this out.

I wait for Mother to say that nothing would induce her to put double-sided sticky stuff anywhere near her Prada linen two-piece, but she smiles, says, "Thank you, Portia," and slaps it on. I don't know why it makes me feel so anxious to see Mother behaving like a normal parent. I always thought I wanted a normal mother, but now that I seem to have one it's really rather unnerving.

"Have you got everything, Angel?" asks Minnie.

"I won't need much," I say. "Not in a nunnery."

"Oh, shush!" says Mercedes. "There's no way you're going to spend your holiday in a nunnery. You're going to spend it on the beach with us and have a fabuloso time." She gives me a little squeeze. It's sweet of her, but I'm not at all sure she's right.

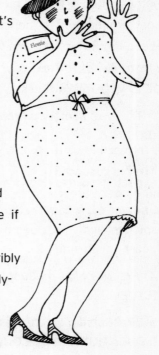

Fearless Flying (and flushed) Flossie

"Angel," says Portia, "do you think Flossie's okay?" Flossie is flapping her passport up and down, fanning her face, which has gone rather pink.

This diverts my attention and we four go over to her to see if everything is all right.

It turns out that Flossie's terribly anxious about flying. She says flying's not natural and if we were meant to fly we would have wings. When finally we get her on to the plane, she wants to know exactly where her life jacket is stored, "just in case." Frankly I couldn't care less if the plane does crash, since my heart is already in smithereens, but I try showing her how to do some yogic breathing to calm her down. Mother and Potty sit on either side of Flossie on the plane. They do their best to reassure her, and as the plane taxis down the runway, Potty gives her an occasional "snifter" of whisky from his hip flask.

By the time we're flying over France, Flossie is singing "My Ol' Man's a Dustman" and blowing kisses to the flight attendant whenever he passes.

The girlies and I are sitting on the other side of the plane. The seats are in twos this side. Minnie and Mercedes are sitting together, with Portia and me sitting behind them. Portia rummages around among the lotions and potions, and cures for this and that in her bag, and finally hands me a piece of paper. *A List of Things to Take Your Mind Off Sydney.* (OOOOHHHHH WOE IS ME.) This includes:

1) *Try to remember all the words to a Madonna song* (BORING).

2) *Name all the states of America* (FUN–NOT–but I expect Mercedes knows most of them).

3) *Paint each fingernail a different color* (BETTER, and she has kindly provided her selection of nail polish for this one).

4) *Practice blowing bubbles with bubble gum provided* (EXCELLENT).

5) *Practice Italian phrases–Phrase book included* (EDUCATIONAL BUT COULD BE FUN).

It's so lovely of her to care about me, especially as neither my parents nor Flossie (who is now sleeping like a baby, with her mouth open) appear to have noticed that I'm still DEVAS-TATED with DISAPPOINTMENT and DESPAIR. Once I've done my nails and blown some spectacularly luscious bubbles, Portia and I settle down with the phrase book. We discover that the "Chow" that Mother keeps coming out with isn't a dog with a black tongue, as Flossie thought, but is spelled "*Ciao*" and it's how you say "Hi" or "Bye" or "Hello" in Italian. When I come to think about it properly, I realize that we all know that "*ciao*" is a really cool way to greet your really cool friends; I just didn't expect Mother to use a cool word like that. The spelling is a bit mystifying, but then, as Flossie would say, it *is* foreign.

By the time the plastic food arrives on its plastic tray I'm feeling miles better. I decide that it would be a bit of a pity if no one but the nuns got to see me in my gorgeous new bikinis. Especially after all the wobble-defying exercise on Cruel Shorts Day (which turned out to be almost completely point-less, as Sydney didn't even notice), and I suddenly wish that I had brought a few more clothes with me. By the time I get back from holiday, bronzed and beautiful with three-inch eyelashes (they will definitely grow in the sunshine) and a mane of stripy, tawny-gold hair (might have to resort to chemical help for that one) and a body that would put any top model to shame (Hm, not sure how that's going to happen)—by the time all that's happened Sydney will probably have realized what a muppet he's been, and he'll be waiting on the doorstep of our house with his arms open wide, ready to enfold me and engulf me in a heavenly hug. . . .

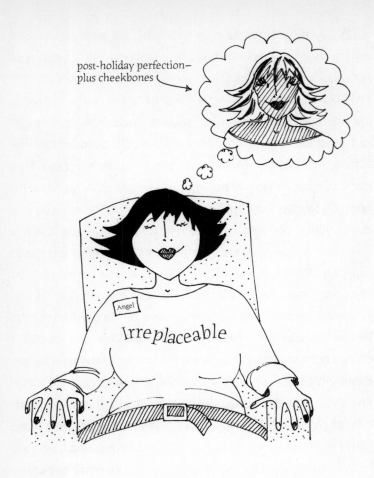

post-holiday perfection—
plus cheekbones

Angel

Irreplaceable

"Angel," says Portia, rudely bursting my bubble gum-pink dream. "For goodness' sake, I've been talking to you for ages. Haven't you heard anything I've said?"

"Er, no," I reply.

"Do you want your piece of chocolate cake?"

"Is that what you ruined my daydream for? Yes, I do," I say attacking it with my plastic fork. "Crumbs, what is Flossie doing? I thought she was asleep."

"Oh, while you were on screen saver, the flight attendant came and asked her if she would like to see the flight deck and meet the captain. She's just coming back now."

"I can see that. But should she be wearing the captain's hat? Flossie," I squeak across the aisle, "what are you doing?"

"Ooooh," she giggles, "I was all of a flutter, and then that nice young man over there . . ." she pauses to wave and blow a kiss to the flight attendant, "came and said, 'Flossie'—he knew my name, isn't that amazing?—"

(Not really, I think, as she's still got the nametag Portia made her stuck on her chest.)

". . . 'the captain would like to meet you.' So off I went. You wouldn't believe how clever he is, Angel! All those dials and switches, and he said he'd NEVER crashed a SINGLE plane . . . Well, I can tell you, a body feels so much safer knowing that!"

Portia wants to ask her what the rather tasty flight attendant's name is, but Flossie's new best friend starts to make an announcement. He tells us that we are beginning our descent (Potty pretends to think he said "descant," and starts singing loudly in his best falsetto, until Mother shushes him) and that we should go back to our seats and put on our seat belts.

Suddenly Flossie looks worried, but we explain to her that we're nearly there and that we are not about to plummet into the sea.

Half an hour later, we have found all our luggage—and each other (no doubt Portia's labels helped)—and are standing at the doors of the airport, waiting in the boiling, bubbling, blistering heat for some transport to take us to Alfie's villa.

Mother is gabbing away to someone. I can't hear what she's saying, because she's too far away, but whatever it is it seems to do the trick and we're shown to a gleaming-white SUV with tinted windows. The driver, who works for Mr. Highead and is apparently called Edu*aaa*rdo, smiles a gleaming-white smile at each of us and we get into the car.

And off we go!

## chapter nine

# Beach Bums and Other Bits

**MY FLABBER HAS** never been so gasted! My gob is beyond smacked! THE VILLA IS TO DIE FOR!!

We've driven for about an hour with Edu*aaa*rdo, who is as cool as the air-conditioning in the SUV, and here we are, at the end of a long tree-lined driveway in front of the gates of paradise. Maybe we had a terrible accident on the way and this is actually heaven?

The car has come to a standstill outside a beautiful honey-colored house. It has elegant, curved windows, with little balconies on the upper floor and the walls are covered with exotic flowers and climbing plants. In the center of the pathway up to the front door there is a fountain in the shape of a fish, blowing out streams of sparkling water. We are all speechless.

Finally Flossie is the first to break the silence, and brings us all back down to earth.

"Well!" she says, "as my grandmother used to say, 'Close your mouth before the flies fly in.' I must say, Mrs. Seepy, I never would have believed that even Mr. Highead would have a place like this . . . And this his SECOND home, too! Well, I never!"

"*Spettacolo* . . ." sighs Mother.

"Smasherooni!" bellows Potty.

We girls just gawk. Eduardo opens the car doors and ushers us out. We offer to carry our cases, but Eduardo seems determined to bring in all the luggage himself. I'm beginning to feel really sorry for him as we watch him lug Mother's fourth suitcase out of the back of the car, but he notices me watching and gives me a spectacular smile. Another young (and possibly rather tasty, but I'm too heartbroken to notice properly) man comes out of the villa to help.

The young man says something, to which Mother answers "*Ciao*," and Portia and I, feeling mightily proud of ourselves, say "*Ciao*" too. Adorable (actually, his name turns out to be Antonio, pronounced Antoooownio, but Adorable suits him better) then babbles on in Italian and Mother translates for us . . .

"He says welcome and how delightful that you girls speak Italian."

I pull in my stomach and think that I might manage the whisper of a smile . . . then I realize, MOTHER TRANSLATED FROM ITALIAN . . . When did she learn to speak Italian?

This is all seriously impressive. This is my Mother, who never has time to do anything in between wafting around and having beauty treatments . . . How come she can speak Italian? I decide that she probably learned when she was young, sometime in the 1920s, or possibly, just possibly, she's been having lessons. This might account for some of the time she's been spending away from home.

Minnie pulls at my arm and whispers in my ear, "Do you think we can go and explore?"

"Yeah," I say, and, leaving the crumblies (plus two cuties, namely Antonio and Eduardo) to sort themselves and our luggage out, we four girlies bound off like cheerful puppies into the villa.

"WOW!" We all gasp, louder and louder as we rush from one blinding room to another. I have never seen anything so . . . so WOW in my entire life. Everything is painted in pale colors and there are huge soft rugs and awesome chandeliers. Upstairs the bedrooms are *spettacolo*. The most spettacololy pukka, which I suppose will have to be Mother and Potty's room, has a colossal four-poster bed and its own balcony from which you can look down over the swimming pool and beyond to the sea.

Flossie will have the room next to theirs. Both rooms have their own bathrooms with marble showers and jacuzzi baths with huge, gold dolphin-head taps. Our bedrooms are on the other side of the villa. We could have one each, but they are all vast and we think that we would be dead lonely that way, so we decide to share two rooms that open into each other—cozy. We also share a bathroom.

"Well, bling bling," says Mercedes. "Old man Midas has certainly touched a few things in here!"

EVERYTHING in the bathroom is either gold or mirrored. The bath is big enough for all of us to use at once, and to prove it we climb into the empty tub and sit with our legs over the edge while we look at ourselves reflected from every angle in the mirrors. This could be horrifying, but luckily my wobble factor isn't completely off the scale. (This must be due to the

massive amount of training before Cruel Shorts Day.)

We bounce around on the beds for a bit before tootling downstairs again. We find Potty sitting on a beautiful rattan chair on a huge patio at the back of the villa. There are soft cushions to sit on and shady umbrellas to keep off the sun. Potty's looking rather wistful.

"Are you all right?" I ask.

"Oh, little Cherub, I just can't help thinking how much old Stinks would love this garden. Look! There's a lizard—he would have had such a jolly time barking at it. Oh dear . . ."

I give Potty a big kiss, and suggest that he write Stinker a postcard. This seems to cheer him up.

We move on through the beautiful grounds. Down below the patio is the poooooooool!

"It hasn't got any edges," squeaks Minnie, and it really

doesn't look as though it has. It's colossal, and the water sort of runs over the sides so that it looks as though the pool goes straight on into the sea. We go around to the other side of the pool, to try to see how it works, but from there we can see down to the beach, and that's even more interesting.

Although it's about six in the evening, there are still people down on the sand, lying like toasted almonds on their brightly colored beach towels.

"Gosh!" says Portia. "Look at that!" And we all strain our necks to see where she's looking.

"Crumpets!" I say as I catch sight of the heavenly body below us. "Is that a Diet Coke break or what??" Not, of course, that I'm really impressed by the tastily tanned heavenly hunk who's doing push-ups on the sand. "What a poser!" I add quickly—although it *is* quite nice to be distracted from my misery.

mirrored sunglasses

stallion's medallion

don't even <u>think</u> further than this

diamond ring

"I suppose you could call him that," says Mercedes as Heavenly Hunk stands upright and waves in our direction. "He's certainly wearing a posing pouch all right!"

Minnie and Portia have already collapsed into a heaving pile of laughter by the side of the pool.

"Don't look!" I squeal. "It's DISGUSTING . . ."

"I bet it's a PPP," Mercedes manages to gasp.

"What's a PPP?" I ask, crossing my legs so as not to have a ghastly giggling PPP accident of my own.

"A Padded Posing Pouch!" shrieks Mercedes.

"Quick," I splutter, "get out of sight—what if he invites himself over?"

"What if who invites himself over, may I ask?" says Flossie, who has waddled up on us unawares. She peers down to the beach then explodes, "Lor lummiducks! Heavens to Betsy! I told Mrs. Seepy that abroad is no place to bring impressionable young girls to. I don't know, I'm sure. You girls look the other way or, better still, come back to the villa and unpack your cases before supper."

We traipse after her, still snorting with "unseemly" laughter.

I begin to feel more and more excited as we unpack our cases. I know that my entire life is in ruins, but now that I'm here and the "scenery" looks so promising I might as well make the most of it. It's so unbelievably hot and the sky is so blue that it's going to be very difficult not to be the tiniest bit happy now and then.

As I pull out my new bikinis and try to decide which of the many drawers to keep them in, I'm suddenly filled with dread at the thought of Mother seeing me in a bikini. She's bound to make some nasty comment about my size. Then I remember that she hasn't been rude about my body for ages. In fact, I can't even recall when she last heaved a huge sigh as I had a third helping of potatoes. Perhaps it's just that she's been out so much lately that she hasn't had time. Or perhaps she really is ill and is losing her memory—she's forgotten that she's in despair about my body. Or maybe I'm tiny now and I haven't noticed? I go and look at myself in the bathroom mirror . . . no, that's definitely not it. I must talk to Flossie about Mother again. There must be something that they're not telling me.

I decide that my bikinis look best draped over the chair by the dressing table. Then I realize that I haven't really brought much else to wear: I've got the pair of jeans that I came in, another pair of jeans, two tops, and two wraps. Golly, what am I actually going to wear when I'm not on the beach? Oh well, I think, I'll have to worry about that in the morning. Now I decide to find Flossie and Food. . . .

"Let's go and have supper," I tell Portia, who has just finished putting her things away.

"Do you think it would be all right if I called my mum first?" asks Portia. "I just want to make sure that she's okay."

"Yeah, I'm sure it would be okay. Let's go and see if we can find the phone." (We were all forbidden to bring our cell phones with us, as they are mega, mega expenny to use from abroad.)

We finally sniff out the telephone, but, annoyingly, Mother is using it. She is laughing and when she sees us she waves a hand at us to shoo us away. I wonder who she can be talking to. Mother doesn't do laughter.

"Bum," I say. "Never mind, Portia, let's find the kitchen. We can come back to use the phone later."

Eventually we find the kitchen. It's awesomely gorgeous with a long table in the center. The table is piled high with fab-colored vegetables and fruit, and whole salamis and all sorts of other exotica, which I'm desperate to investigate. But Flossie is standing on one side of the table, glaring fiercely at an attractive, dark-haired woman, who is standing at the other side of the table staring back at her.

*girlie laugh*

*Prada belt*

*Manolo made these specially for Mother*

"Hello, Flossie," I say, to break the silence. "Wuzzup?" Usually when I do my mega-cool hip-hop lingo Flossie tells me to "speak the Queen's English," but this time she doesn't move, or speak or even BLINK.

"Flossie?" I try again.

Flossie humphs.

Then the woman on the other side of the table starts gabbing away in Italian, and waving her arms around and pointing to the things on the table.

Flossie turns to us and says, "SEE? I don't know what a

94

body's supposed to do. I mean, how am I going to make a nice, comforting shepherd's pie out of this lot, and with HER shouting at me all the time. I'm sure I don't know . . ."

"But Flossie," I say. "You're supposed to be having a bit of a holiday. You don't have to do all the cooking."

"Well, I'm not having just ANYONE cook for you all," she says. Her eyes are filling with tears, so I rush over to put my arms around her. But before I can get to her the plump, dark-haired woman does the same thing! There we are, all three of us together in a sort of bundle, swaying and crying and shouting, and none of us knowing what the heck's going on. I look desperately around to Portia, who looks as gobsmacked as me. I wonder if this is an old Italian custom, and if so, what we are supposed to do next.

Mother to the rescue! She must have heard the commotion from the little telephone room, and has teetered along to see what all the noise is about. I don't know what it is with Mother on this holiday, but she has suddenly become terribly useful.

Mother calms everyone down. With a bit more arm waving and her mysteriously acquired Italiano, she manages to explain to Flossie and Maria (pronounced Marrria, with those sort of motorbike-sounding *R*s in the middle) that they are to work TOGETHER in the kitchen, and suggests that perhaps Maria could help Flossie make some of the local specialties.

"*Ecco!*" says Maria, giving Flossie a big hug. "*Va bene?*"

Flossie looks at Mother. Mother says, "Say 'yes,' Flossie. Maria wants to be friends. The word for yes is '*Si.*'"

"Oh," says Flossie, wiping the tears away with her apron. "Yessi."

Flossie
flummoxed

Marrrria

wish I'd
brought
something
cooler to
wear

I take a moment to look hard at Mother. I don't think I can be right about her being ill—she looks amazing.

"Is everything all right, Mother?" I ask.

"Perfectly," she says and BLOWS ME A KISS. . . .

# chapter ten

# Sunscreen Scream and Frizzling Frisbees

**WE HAD A WOWZER** supper last night! It was totally fabulouso. Maria and Flossie cooked like demons, and between them (with a little help in the tasting department from yours truly) they produced the best pasta with meatballs and tomato sauce that has ever been tasted this side of *Paradiso*—even JONC, Superstar and Broken Heart Soother, would have been impressed. Before the pasta we had something called Auntie Pasta, which actually didn't have any pasta in it at all. It was lots of different types of salami and fantastic olive-oily sun-dried tomatoes and other grilled veggies, with the most DELICIOUS crunchy, fresh bread.

Mother, Potty, Flossie, and Maria all drank red wine and Flossie got all pink and giggly and did her Spanish dance thing around the table. Mother did try to explain to her that we were in the wrong country for castanet clacking, but that didn't stop her. Maria joined in, but first she took the hairpins out of her bun so that her hair was all streaming behind her as she leaped around the kitchen.

Potty kept shouting that it was all "Jollyo supero!" and Mother just smiled.

Everyone was very quiet at breakfast this morning and Maria had to make Flossie a rose-water compress to put on her forehead, because she said she was feeling a bit "topsy turvy."

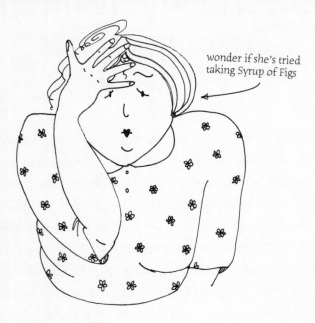

wonder if she's tried taking Syrup of Figs

"So which is it to be?" asks Minnie. "The pink one or the black one?"

I'm feeling full of hope this morning. I'm convinced that my holiday makeover idea is going to turn me from dull, ordinary, everyday Angel into fab, sun-kissed, *gorgioso* Angel, who is going to go home and stun Sydney into total adoration.

"I'm going to go for the pink," I say. "I think the Italian Stallions with Medallions are ready for a flash of my Heavenly

Hip-hugging Harrods Haute Couture!" I whiz into the bathroom and slip into my slinky new bikini. I don't look in the mirrors at all. I don't want to spoil the beautiful feeling that I woke up with this morning.

"Well, strike me senseless! Am I gorgeous OR WHAT?" I shout as I leap out of the bathroom . . . Then I see my three bestest, fabbiest friends all looking to die for divine. Suddenly I'm not sure the pink bikini is such a good idea, now that I'm reminded of who I'll be lying next to on the beach. I try to put a brave face on things as I pack all the different sunscreens we've brought with us into my beach bag. Then I swathe myself in my pink (toning and color coordinated) beach wrap, put on my spectacular sun specs and I'm ready to go.

"Do you think I ought to take my toilet-seat covers with me?" asks Portia and I suddenly realize that what with all the excitement with the clash of the cooks last night I forgot to ask her how her mum was when she spoke to her.

"Oh, she said that she's feeling much better now," says Portia. "She said that there is nothing to worry about. But I still do, you know, worry . . ."

"Well, you mustn't," says Mercedes. "If she's told you not to, you must do your best to have a lovely time."

"Okay . . ." says Portia reluctantly. But then, with a big grin, "Let's go!"

We scamper off across the garden, passing Potty on the way. Potty is holding a bright pink plastic basket and he tells us that he's waiting for "the girls" (the WHO? Does he mean Maria and Flossie?), who are going to take him to the market with them. "Promised Alfie that I would carry out some in-depth research

99

into all the different types of pasta and salami that you can find down here. Old Stinks would have loved the market . . ." he says wistfully. "I sayo," he adds, "You all look jolly jollyo. Going off to the beach? Super dupero. See you all later."

"Okay," we all say, "bye."

"Byio," shouts Potty as we disappear into the wild blue yonder—well, toward the beach actually.


And WHAT a beach it is! Miles of pale, gold sand and sparkling sea. AND, wherever you look, Beautiful, Bronzed, Perfect Size-Eight Bodies . . . Oh no! I'm never going to be able to unwrap myself from my color-coordinated beach wrap and reveal my economy-size body with its tabby-cat-striped legs. Not with all these TINY people everywhere. And especially not when every Eyetalian Eye seems to be looking in our direction.

"What's the prob, babes?" asks Mercedes as she peels off her skintight jeans to reveal more of her skintight, tight skin in its glam new bikini.

"Oh, nothing," I say, trying to sound nonchalant.

"Come on then, take your cover-up off," giggles Minnie as she reveals her cutesy wootsie red and white polka-dot bikini.

"Don't be shy," says Portia as she shimmies out of her T-shirt and shorts, before spreading out her gleaming white beach towel under the umbrella.

Well, at least no one's going to look at ME now, but I still feel wobbly.

"I can't," I say. 'I've just remembered that I promised Sydney I'd call him this morning . . . I'd better go and do that now . . . bye."

"Angelica Cookson Potts, you lying little toad," giggles Minnie. "You never promised anything of the kind. And besides, Sydney is history, isn't he?"

"No, he isn't," I say hotly. "I know there's still hope."

The girlies all stare at me, but they don't say anything.

"I don't think I feel well. I think I might have caught whatever Flossie had this morning. I think I'd better go and lie down. . . ."

"You can't catch a hangover," says Portia. "Now take your wrap off and stop being daft. You look wonderful . . . Come on."

"Okay," I say. "Here goes."

Obviously I can't unwrap in full view of everyone. Especially not with an Eyetalian still eyeing me up from the other side of the paddle boats. I lie down fully wrapped and sort of wriggle myself out of my wrappings. I was planning to lie on my beach wrap, but it's very difficult to get it straight while I'm lying on it. I flap about a bit and finally get myself sorted. Hey, this is not so bad, I think. I'll just lie here with my eyes shut and then I won't know if anyone is laughing at me or not. Then I realize that I haven't put any sunscreen on. I stretch my arm as far as I can across the sand toward my beach bag. Knickers! I can't . . . quite . . . reach . . . it . . .

"Mercedes," I say, in my most wheedling voice, "do you think you could get up and bring me my bag? Please . . . pretty please!"

"You so have to be joking," says Mercedes with a laugh. "I've just got comfortable. You get up and get it—it's on your side."

"Oh . . . Minnie?" I begin, in my sweetest girlie voice, but before I can even ask her she's said, "No."

I lie still for a bit and will the beach bag to come closer. It doesn't. I try rolling over onto my tummy and reaching out from that way up, but all that happens is that my top gets in a muddle and when I look down I see that one of my boobs has almost escaped from its pink boulder-holder. I adjust myself and sigh loudly.

"Angel, for goodness' sake," says Portia. "Just get up and get your bag, and stop being such a ninny."

Okay then, I think, I will.

I stand up slowly, checking all the while that everything is safely tucked in place. All right so far. I smooth my hair, pull in my stomach and lean, bravely forward to pick up my beach bag. As I straighten up my eyes wander across the sand . . . and meet the eyes of Mr. PPP!! I'm frozen to the spot and not in a tremendously flattering position, either. Mr. PPP is in the middle of his push-up routine. I was so busy worrying about my body that I hadn't noticed him on the beach beside us. He gives me a beaming smile and says, *"Ciao, bellissima!"*

Well! I'm flat on the sand, with my eyes tight shut and my beach bag clutched in my hand, quicker than you could jangle a medallion!

I don't dare open my eyes again for what feels like hours,

but I'm getting totally freaked by the thought of lying there without my Factor 40 so I very gently turn my head in the direction of the Prince of Push-ups and squint through my waterproof lash-thickening mascara . . . I can't see him. I open my eyes properly . . . PHEW! He's nowhere in sight. I'm so relieved! I sit up to rub on the sunscreen.

"What was all that about?" asks Portia.

OhmyGod!

"He called me "*bellissima*." What does it mean?" I ask, knowing pretty much exactly what it means, but needing to hear someone else say it.

"It means he thinks you're beautiful," sighs Mercedes. "How romantic!"

"Mr. PPP? URGH! I don't think so," I say, but am feeling well flattered nevertheless. I continue slapping on the Factor 40, hoping that it will help even out the tabby effect, and gaze around the beach. These Italians are seriously glam. They're all so dark and exotic-looking. Maybe I won't go blonde and streaky after all.

I notice Mercedes scribbling away on a pad of pale pink paper. "What are you doing?" I ask.

"I'm writing to Paul," she says. "I promised him I'd write him a letter every day. Do you think Maria might show me where to mail it?"

"Ahhh!" we all sigh together. Now that really is romantic!

"What are you guys going to do about boyfriends while we're here?" Mercedes asks.

"Well, obviously I'm waiting to get back to Sydney," I say.

The others exchange glances and Minnie says, "Angel . . ." in a warning sort of way.

I ignore them.

"I think I'll wait and see if George's friend Jimmie might like to take me out when we get back," says Minnie, changing the subject. "Will they be home by then?"

"Yeah, I think so," I say. "I'll get George to bring him around."

"Well, I'm jolly well going to have a holiday romance," says Portia, "even if none of you stick-in-the-muds are going to join me . . . He won't be Italian, obviously. I mean, I have to be able to talk to him . . . Although, I must say, some of those boys over there look quite interesting . . ."

"Portia," we all squeal. "You sly thing. You've been checking out the hot spots on the sand when we all thought your eyes were closed!"

"I don't think much of that one on the left," she continues. "He doesn't look as if he washes much. That one with the dark curly hair looks pretty yummy—but he's probably Italian."

We all peer over to the group of boys who are playing frisbee a few yards away.

"Mmmm," says Mercedes, "I see what you meeeeEEEEEEKKK . . ."

The Frisbee comes frizzing over in our direction and lands
slap in Portia's lap . . . was this the Fickle Finger of Fate, or
what?

Curly comes cantering over to Portia. "I'm so sorry," he says—
in ENGLISH. "Did it hurt you?"

"Nnno," says Portia. "I'm fine." And hands the Frisbee back
to Curly.

"You're not bruised or anything? I've got some cream in my
bag if you need it?"

curly

getting
ready for
LURVE

The rest of us gaze at them in stunned silence. I don't think Curly has even noticed us.

"Have you?" asks Portia, a little breathlessly. "I've got some in my bag, too. I always carry a few remedies with me wherever I go."

"That's amazing—so do I," says Curly. "My parents are homeopathic doctors so I expect that's why I've always got a cure for everything."

"MY parents are doctors too," squeaks Portia.

"No!" says Curly. "My name's Jack, by the way. What's yours?"

And that's it. Mercedes and Minnie and I might just as well sink into the sand for all the notice they take of us. Jack throws the Frisbee back to his friends, who carry on playing without him. He plonks himself down on the sand next to Portia and, with barely a glance in our direction, they begin an in-depth discussion about all things medical. And as they agree on the nastiness of anything germy, the little flower of romance begins to blossom.

# Monstrously Marvelous Meatballs
# in Tomato Sauce

## MEATBALLS

2 slices bread

1 lb really tip-top quality ground beef

½ lb pork sausage meat

½ green pepper, finely chopped

1 egg, beaten

1 medium-sized onion, very finely chopped

1 large garlic clove, crushed

1 small bunch fresh oregano or ½ tsp dried oregano

1 tbsp chopped fresh parsley

1 tbsp tomato puree

salt and freshly ground black pepper

1 rounded tbsp plain flour

1 tbsp and ½ tsp olive oil

## SAUCE

1 small onion, chopped

½ a green pepper, chopped

14 oz. can Italian (of course) tomatoes, or 1 lb fresh, ripe tomatoes, chopped

1 garlic clove, crushed

1 tbsp fresh basil, chopped or 1 tsp of dried basil

---

Heat the oven to 375°.

Cut the crusts off the bread and break it up into crumbs. Put the bread crumbs into a bowl with all the other meatball ingredients and season with salt and black pepper. Use your hands to squidge the ingredients together until they're evenly mixed.

Take a little blob of the mixture (about a tablespoon) and shape it into a ball. Repeat until all this mixture is used up (this should make about 16 to 18 meatballs). Put the flour on a plate and roll each meatball in the flour, until they are well coated. Heat half of the oil in a large frying pan and gently fry the meatballs until they are light brown. Put the browned meatballs into a casserole dish and set aside.

In the same frying pan as you used to fry the meatballs, heat the remaining oil and soften the onion and the pepper. (This means frying them over a low heat until they are soft, but not brown. It will take about 5 minutes.) Add the tomatoes, garlic, and basil and simmer the sauce for a couple of minutes. Taste the sauce and add more salt or pepper if you think it needs it.

When you're happy with the sauce, pour it over the meatballs. Put a lid on the casserole dish and place it in the oven. Cook for 45 minutes, then take the lid off the casserole and cook for another 15 to 20 minutes.

Flossie and Maria served their meatballs with homemade spaghetti, but they would be scrummy with any type of pasta.

This makes enough for 4 hungry people.

## chapter eleven

# Curious Customs and Bottoms Up!

**I'VE LOST ALL** track of time—most of the days are pretty much the same. We girlies spend every morning on the beach. Jack is always there, and he and Portia discuss medical matters and get friendly. There's a really drippy English boy who's got the hots for Minnie. He bought her an ice cream yesterday, and as he was presenting it to her he dropped it in the sand. I did feel quite sorry for him because Minnie couldn't stop giggling. He looks like a real geek. He's got red peeling shoulders and he wears socks with his sandals. I mean, for goodness' sake, even *Potty* doesn't do that!

Mr. PPP is also always on the beach, and somehow or other he

bet his mum chose these for him

strawberry and vanilla —shame

goofy geek

always manages to find a spot somewhere near us. He's got a whole gang of Italian Stallion friends and they all wave and say *"Ciao, bella!"* to ME every morning. They don't even seem to notice Minnie, Mercedes, or Portia. I would quite like it if I felt they were admiring me—it might make me feel better about Sydney—but I expect they're laughing at me and talking about me in Italian, saying what a chubby chick I am and wondering why I've got tabby-cat stripy legs. I get totally embarrassed and I have to roll over on to my tummy, close my eyes, and hope they will go away. This means that my back is getting way browner than my front.

We always come back to the villa for lunch. Mother is always out, no one knows where. After we've all eaten, Potty and Flossie sit with us under the huge umbrella on the patio. We girlies watch Adorable Antonio as he ripples around the garden, clipping hedges and watering flowers. So far, Flossie hasn't appeared in her bathing suit. She always thinks of a good excuse when we suggest that she come swimming with us.

Today, we're all lying in the shade after a delicious meal of huge fresh tomatoes and mozzarella cheese with a drizzle of oil and a sprinkling of chopped fresh basil leaves. (JONC would just love all these fresh ingredients.) Potty is writing a report titled "Pastas are Like Puddles—They Come in All Shapes and Sizes." Flossie is snoozing. Mother is not around, as usual, and I am getting worryingly worried about her. I mean, I know that there's a Gucci outlet in the local super-smart town, but she can't be there ALL the time, can she? The more I think about Mother, the more that little tiny worry in the back of my mind starts to niggle at me . . . I wonder if it could be possible . . .

Could she . . . Would she . . . Might she . . . BE HAVING AN AFFAIR?

I think back to that time in London when I overheard her talking to someone called Filippo on the phone. Filippo is an Italian name, I realize. What if this Filippo person has come to Italy, too, and that's why Mother is never around? She could be with HIM. And that time when we were walking to Horrids to buy the Love Hearts and I asked the girlies if they thought Mother was acting strangely Minnie said that perhaps she was having an affair . . . I *know* she was only joking. I thought at the time that she was completely bonkers and had obviously been watching way too many TV dramas. *Of course* she was joking . . . But what if Minnie was actually *right*? WHAT IF MOTHER IS HAVING AN AFFAIR?

I don't know what to do. I look at Potty. Does he suspect? Poor Potty! I can't ask him. I know it's hard to imagine anyone actually being IN LOVE with Potty (although he used to be quite handsome about a hundred years ago, when he was young), but he and Mother get on really well. I know they don't do everything together, but they always look happy when they *are* together. They both love opera and they often go out to parties and things. And Mother must love Potty because she stuck with him even when it looked as if he might go to prison during the haggis ordeal.

I look over at Flossie. I'd like to ask her what she thinks, but decide that she has enough of her own problems, what with buying provisions in a foreign language and coming to grips with "sun-dried this and marinated that and at least four-hundred different types of pasta." She says she "can't get a proper sausage ANYWHERE!" It could be too much for her to think about now. No, I decide that I'll have to keep my suspicions to myself. I'll have to be CERTAIN before I tell anyone.

Anyway, I tell myself, perhaps there's a perfectly innocent explanation for Mother's behavior. I mean, this is my mother—not some Marilyn Monroe sex kitten. I mean, MOTHER having an affair . . . EHEW!! The sun must be affecting my brain . . .

Having decided that I'm probably imagining the whole thing, I realize that at least Mother is sure to be here this evening because we've all been invited to a "drinkies do" before dinner at a local *palazzo* with some Italian friends of Alfie's. Apparently, any friend of Alfie's is a friend of ours.

"Oh, crikey!" I say, sitting up and shattering the peace of the afternoon. "What on earth am I going to wear to this drinks thing this evening? I haven't brought any clothes with me. I was meant to be joining a nunnery, and now that I haven't I'm stuck without so much as a SCRAP of evening wear!"

"Don't worry," says Minnie lazily. "We'll lend you something."

"Maria says she is going to lend ME something to wear," says Flossie, snortling out of her slumbers. "She says she's got just the thing."

Flossie starts giggling to herself and I'm left wondering: (a) how I could possibly borrow anything of Minnie's when she's so petite she barely comes up to my elbow, and (b) how could Flossie and Maria have had a conversation about party clothes when neither speaks the other's language?

I try to stay calm and think of something else. I close my

eyes thinking that I'll have a little daydream about Sydney and how much he's
missing me. I stretch out on my cush-
ioned mat and wait for the bliss to begin.

But when I try to think about
Scintillating Syd, a picture of Mother
with the mysterious Filippo keeps
rising up in my mind, and somehow
won't go away so I make a quick
change of plan.

CRUMBS!

"Girlieeees?" I begin, trying my best
to sound really sweet.

There's a groan from the others.

"Do you think we could go and look
through all your things to find little
Angelly-pops somefing soooper to wear this
evening? She soooo doesn't want to look like
a doggy woggy at the drinkie do tonight."

There's another, louder, groan.

"And if you're reeeely sweeetie weeetie girlies, Angelly-
pops might make you all some of JONC, Superstar's, oh-so-
Italian, orange and polenta biccies for tea."

There's a very gratifying scuffle as the girlies get to their
feet. "Okay," says Mercedes. "Come on, let's go and style
Angel. Tell you what, why don't you go and make the biscuits
while we go and put together an amazing outfit for you?
Then when you've finished making the biccies you can come
and try it all on."

I'm not sure about this.

"You wouldn't just let me make the biscuits while you do nothing, would you?"

"Course not," says Portia, and even though Minnie is giggling, I suppose I believe them.

So off I go to mix and bake, while they go off in the other direction to plan some top togs for me to wear.

I make the glorious little golden biscuits, stick them on a plate and hotfoot it upstairs to see what the girlies have put together for me to wear.

I love this— wonder if I ought to use some double-sided tape just in case

I completely and utterly love my friends! There, draped divinely over my bed, is a scrumptious selection of super style. They've taken one of the wraps that Mercedes's parents bought for her in India, and tied it so that it looks like one of those totally IN halter-neck dresses. It's fantastic material—all hot clashing colors, with mirrored sparkly bits in a pattern along the edges. They've put out a pair of Portia's shoes (my feet are the only bits of me that are any-where near the same size as anything of Portia's), which are spiky-heeled and sparkly-toed. Then there's one of Minnie's many pairs of dangly earrings and even a little embroidered bag that she made herself.

I'm worried that the beautiful wrap won't wrap far enough around me. I feel sure that some of my wobble will flollop out at the edges. But Minnie is so clever with her knotting that when I've got it on nothing flollops at all. In fact, the fabric *skims over* the worst of the wobbly bits and I almost look quite SLIM.

"Well, as Flossie would say, I'm going to look the bee's knees!" I say breezily.

By the time we've eaten all the biscuits, and done lots of getting-ready things, I've managed to stop thinking about Mother, and I feel pretty perky and ready to party!

Mother wafts back in time to change into her evening dress. She looks fabulous, as usual. And so does Flossie—she's wearing a bright-pink dress with the top three buttons UNDONE and a rose behind her ear!! I've never seen Flossie in anything, but her "sensible" shirtwaist dresses.

"Splendido!" says Potty, when he sees her. "What a lucky chappie I am to have so many gorgeoso women to escort!" I'm sure all the women feel they're just as lucky to have Potty to escort them. He's wearing his pale-blue-and-white-striped pajama trousers and linen jacket, topped off with his old panama hat.

Eduardo is driving us to the *palazzo*. He winks at me as I get into the SUV. I can't stop blushing. I wait for him to wink at the girlies. He doesn't.

The *palazzo* is splendido indeedo and Alfie's friends are very welcoming. In fact, the host babbles away to Mother, and

Action Man plastic hair

Paolo
Pinchadibottomi

should I have
pinned a "do not
disturb" notice on
my bottom?

winkle-pickers

keeps pointing to me and saying, "*Bella, bella!* Youra daughter
she is a *bellissima!*" Excuse me, but this is *me* he's talking
about! Me, wrapped up in someone else's wrap, with my wobble
factor teetering on the edge of out of control. He doesn't say
the others are "*bellissima.*" He leads me across the room and
introduces me in his excellent English to a very nice couple who
are both chefs from London on holiday. I really like chatting
with them, but I want to find the girlies and I can't see them
anywhere. I can't seem to get away, but finally I manage to

excuse myself, saying that I'm going to try some more of the delicious little nibbles.

As I'm walking past a group of men on my way to get another deliciouso Parma ham munchy, one of the men surreptitiously leans forward and PINCHES MY BOTTOM!! I don't know what to do . . . What are you supposed to say when someone has just pinched your bottom? Thank you? How kind of you? Do that again and I'll slosh you? Is this a compliment or an insult? I want to go home NOW!

I scurry off, with my face as pink as Flossie's dress, to try and find Mother. I must tell her what happened and ask her to go and tell that leery letch that he is NOT to pinch me again. I see her on the other side of the room. But is that happy, laughing, relaxed-looking person over there truly my mother? I'm spellbound by the sight of her. I can't make myself go over and interrupt her when she's having such fun.

I look at her closely. Is this the face of a woman who's having an affair? OOOOOOOh! I think it might be. Why else would she look so different? So RADIANT? What am I going to do? AND WHAT ABOUT POTTY??

I look across to him. He's having a very loud conversation (in English with plenty of arm waving) with Signora Palazzo (our hostess). I wonder how he can be so blind. I mean, anyone with half a brain cell could see that Mother is acting really strangely. When did she last risk having a really good laugh? She's forever telling us that laugh lines are no laughing matter. Maybe this Filippo person is here, I think. I wonder what he looks like? I watch mother carefully for a while, but I can't see her making eyes at anyone in particular. I feel awful. What if

Mother really is having an affair? Perhaps if I tell Flossie about my fears she'll know what to do. But where is she?

By the time I find her, everyone is leaving. "Who have you been talking to all evening, Flossie?" I ask, wondering how I'm going to show her that I need a private word.

"Oh," she squawks, "I feel like the cat who got the cream . . . I met such a nice man who really cut the mustard . . . I've been in a proper pickle and he's going to sort the wheat from the chaff . . ."

"What are you talking about, Flossie?"

"What I am talking about, young lady," says Flossie, "is my new friend, Mr. Fruity-Men-Oh-No. He's a grocer and he says he can show me exactly where to buy PROPER sausages!"

It's no good. I can see that I won't get any sense out of Flossie now, not when she's found a holiday replacement for Diggory. What is it about Italy and romance? Everyone seems to be falling in love. There's Flossie and her grocer, Portia and Jack, and Mother and her mystery man . . . Not me, of course— I was already in love when we arrived . . . Maybe it's a good thing that I'm being distracted by Mother and the bottom pinching—at least I'm not thinking about Sydney.

I don't feel like talking in the car going home. The girlies are telling us all about Signor and Signora Palazzo's daughters, who they spent the evening chatting with. Then Flossie starts on about Mr. Fruity-Men-Oh-No. Mother laughs. (Yes, she properly laughs.) "Flossie," she says, "you *are* priceless! Your friend was a '*fruttivendolo*', which is the Italian word for 'greengrocer' . . . It isn't his name!"

Suddenly I see red. "Isn't it amazing how WONDERFUL your

Italian is, Mother? I can't THINK how you could possibly have learned so quickly. Unless of course you had an Italian friend to PRACTICE with."

"Thank you, Angel," says Mother, completely missing my sarcasm. "I'm hoping to make some Italian friends. Just like Flossie."

"Oh," says Flossie, adjusting the rose behind her ear. "I'm sure you're right about my friend's name, Mrs. Seepy, but to me he will always be my Mr. Fruity-Men-Oh-No!"

Everyone laughs except me. "What's up, Angel?" asks Mercedes, who is always the first to notice if anyone isn't happy.

"Oh, I don't know," I say, wondering what I can say that will sound convincing. Then I remember the terrible thing that happened to me at the party. "It's just that some creepy creep PINCHED MY BOTTOM while I was escaping from a couple of really nice, but quite old people. I was looking for you guys when it happened and I was so embarrassed that I didn't know what to do. You were all busy chatting and having fun while I was trying to avoid leaving my bottom anywhere it might get tweaked. It was SO horrible . . ."

Potty is outraged and says that Italian men are "simply not British." He's quite upset, until Mother points out that although botty pinching isn't something we think of as appropriate, in Italy it is meant as a friendly compliment. She says that I should try not to be too upset about it.

I wanted to ask Mother if that was how Filippo won her over—by pinching her bottom. I couldn't do it though, not in front of Potty.

* * *

119

Much later, after we have had our supper out on the terrace under the stars and are all in our rooms getting ready to go to bed, Mercedes asks me again, "Are you still really upset about the pinching thing, Angel? You don't look very happy."

And then it all comes flooding out: "Oh, no! It's not the pinching thing, it's Mother!"

"What do you mean?" asks Minnie. "Your Mother looks so well and happy!"

"No, no," I say. "It's not about her having an illness. It's . . . it's . . . about her HAVING AN AFFAIR!"

"WHAT??" they all say in unison, goggling at me in disbelief.

"Angel, you're mad," said Mercedes. "Why would your Mother be having an affair? She's got Potty . . . And she . . . she wouldn't—your mother's not like that . . ."

They go on and on, trying to reassure me, and eventually I feel calm enough to go to bed. I fall asleep, but wake up in the middle of the night and lie with my eyes wide open, wondering if they are right.

# Parma Ham Palazzo Wraps

1 8 oz. container sour cream
3 tomato tortillas (large, if
possible)
¼ lb sliced Parma ham
9 leaves spinach, washed

1 avocado, peeled, pitted
and cut into strips
salt and freshly ground
black pepper
juice of 1 lemon

---

Divide each of the ingredients into three so that you have enough
filling for each tortilla. Spread sour cream over each tortilla, then
lay on the slices of ham, the spinach, and the avocado strips.
Season with salt and black pepper and then squeeze a little lemon
juice over the avocado (Flossie says the lemon stops the avocado
from going brown). Roll the tortillas up as tight as you can
without all the filling falling out and cut them into little round
slices, ready to munch when your mouth gets lonely or for parties.

Makes about 30 bite-sized pieces.

## chapter twelve

# Sea View—See Through

**THE NEXT DAY** I try really hard not to think about Mother at all. If my mind does wander off in her direction, I tug it back right away and try to concentrate on the very serious problem of how I am going to get my front as brown as my back. I'm not brave enough to frizzle the flip side when Mr. PPP and his gang are on the beach—they might come and talk to me if I'm faceup.

This morning I can't see them anywhere, so I decide to begin the day with a swim to wash away my worries. The others don't want to come in with me. Portia is discussing natural remedies with Jack, and Mercedes is writing to Paul again. Minnie found a whole stack of magazines in the villa and she is happily trawling through the fashion sections, finding ideas that are just SO next season.

I skip off across the sand. Splish, splash . . . Ah! Lovely—the sea is cool and blue and beautiful. I feel so light and slim in the water. I float about for a bit, squinting up at the brilliant, clear sky through my eyelashes. As I'm deciding that it's time to

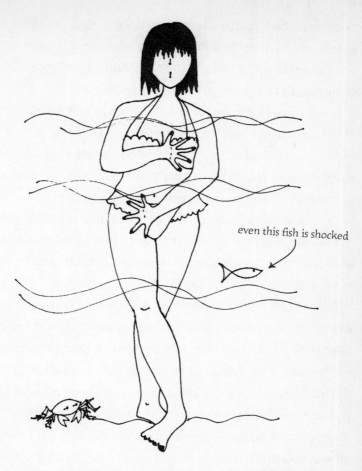

even this fish is shocked

come out and waddle up the beach I have a horrible thought: this is the first time I've swum in my pinkio bikinio, and I'm not at all sure whether it goes see-through when it's wet. I peer down through the water. CRIKEY! There's an awful lot more of me showing than is decent. PANIC! I wish I had brought my towel down to the water with me. I look up the beach to where the girlies are, and try waving to catch their eye. None of them look my way, but some freako with a knotted hanky on his head (must be English) waves back. I'm just about to shout to Minnie when I spot Mr. PPP prancing about on the sand with his Italian-stallion friends. PURPLE PANIC! Now what am I going to do? I can't get out . . .

I have to swim around for HOURS trying to look athletic and fit before Minnie finally comes to ask me if I'm all right.

"No, I am not!" I snort. "This bikini has about as much coverage as sheer foundation. I CAN'T GET OUT. And you haven't so much as glanced in my direction for hours!"

Of course Minnie gets terrible giggles, but at least she goes and fetches my towel. I manage to sort of crawl out of the sea while she holds the towel up for me. I wrap it tightly around me and scamper back up the sand.

"I look like a prune!" I squeak when I finally sit down with the others. "It's the pits that NONE of you noticed that I was in dire need of help." As I do that British thing of changing on the beach under a tent made of beach towels, I see that Mr. PPP isn't around any more. Oh well, at least I can lie on my back for a bit and turn up the tan.

As I'm sloshing the Factor 40 over my stomach (and thinking that four fresh rolls for breakfast might have been a little excessive) Portia and Jack continue their medical confab. Portia is describing her mum's symptoms to Jack. Suddenly a big grin spreads across his face and he asks, "Is your mum ever sick in the morning?"

"Yeeeees . . ." says Portia. "OHMYGOD! SHE'S PREGNANT!!!"

Well, that stops us all in our tracks. Of course, we don't KNOW that this is the reason Portia's mum has been looking so unwell. But we're SURE it is. Minnie and Mercedes and I think

it's utterly fab that Portia might have another little sister or brother. She thinks it's utterly gross.

"My parents are so OLD . . ." she says. "And they're doctors too—surely they know how not to, you know . . . I think it's disgusting . . . they ought to know better at their age . . . EHEW!!! I'm sure you're right though," she goes on. "The more I think about it, the more obvious it is . . . Well, really. What were my parents thinking of?"

Jack tries very hard to make Portia see the happy side of the situation, and they go on and on discussing parents and brothers and sisters and babies while the rest of us get on with lying around and daydreaming.

All this talk of Portia's parents has made me think about Mother again. I realize that I can't just ignore the situation—

I've GOT to find out what's going on. I'm plotting and planning Ways to Find Out What Mother's Doing when Minnie suddenly says, "Oh no, there's that drippy dweeb again . . . It looks as if he's coming this way . . . I think I'll take my inflatable raft and go off for a float." And she bounds off across the beach, with her red raft tucked under her arm.

I lie on my back, willing my stomach to get tanned and TIGHT, and wondering what to do about Mother, while Mercedes reads aloud a quiz from one of the magazines Minnie brought down with her. The quiz is supposed to help us to find out How Attractive We are to Boys. Portia and Jack are still talking doctors so Mercedes and I do the quiz on our own. After fifteen very complicated questions, it turns out that I'm a quiet, shy girl who boys tend to overlook. "Well, that's a pile of poo," I say. "You'd need a stepladder to overlook MEEEE−" I sit up suddenly because I can hear Minnie shouting from somewhere. "Oh, look," I say, "Minnie's waving."

not drowning, just waving

takes a load of
puff to blow one
of these up

We both wave back and are settling back down again when there's a terrific splashing and sploshing, and shouts of, "Don't worry! I'm coming! I'll save you . . ." And we watch open-mouthed as Dynamo Dweeb pulls off his sandals and socks and flings his weedy pink-and-white body into the sea. He splashes out to Minnie and there's a huge commotion as she tries to beat him off. But he won't give up, and finally drags her, still sitting on her raft, back to the shore.

"Blimey," says Mercedes. "This is better than *Baywatch*!"

Minnie is now bounding back up the beach, with Dynamo Dweeb in hot pursuit.

"Let me give you the kiss of life," he pants. "I'm sure you must be breathless after all that struggling to survive. I'm so glad you're alive!"

I expect his mummy loves him

ears blocked

"Of course I'm alive!" shouts Minnie, who is usually such a gentle soul. "And the only thing making me breathless is trying to run away from you!" She comes skidding to a halt at my feet and throws down her raft before plunking herself on top of it. "GO AWAY!" she shouts, really quite rudely, as Dynamo Dweeb arrives. But he decides that she is suffering from shock, and sits down at her feet, from where he gazes at her like a lovesick puppy. Minnie is not impressed. I decide that the only sensible thing to do is to tell him to go "walkies" while we go back to the villa for lunch.

After lunch my tummy starts to feel sort of warm and tingly. By suppertime it's feeling hot and I decide to investigate. I peel off my things in the many-mirrored bathroom and I discover that I must have made a bit of a botch-up with the Factor 40. In fact, I think I must have put aftersun on by mistake, because now my tummy is one big, hot, red blob, and it REALLY, REALLY HURTS.

## chapter thirteen

# Motorbikes, Men . . . and Mother!

**NOT ONLY WAS** my tummy on fire last night, but Mother's eyes seemed to be alight with what I'm sure was the light of love. I couldn't sleep at all. I tossed and turned in my bed and felt hot and sick and miserable.

Mother isn't at breakfast the next morning. Flossie says she had to go out early for an appointment. Well, that's it. I'm going to find out what's going on.

"Flossie," I say, as soon as we are alone and I can muster enough of my courage, "where do you think Mother keeps going all the time?"

"Oh, I've no idea, I'm sure," says Flossie as she tucks a fresh flower in the front of her sundress (bare arms, low back and front with a gathered skirt—yes, this IS Flossie!).

"Well, don't you think it's odd," I continue, "that she's out so often and no one knows where she's going or WHO SHE'S WITH?" I glare at Flossie and raise my eyebrows.

She smiles at me and says, "I'm sure I don't know what you mean."

"I mean," I say, taking a huge gulp of air, "that Mother is obviously HAVING AN AFFAIR."

"Bless my buttons," squawks Flossie, "whatever will you think of next? Now get out of my way and let me get on with making the pasta before Maria gets here. I want to surprise her and have it all finished before she arrives."

And that was it. "Whatever will you think of next?," as if I'm imagining the whole thing. But I KNOW that I'm not.

I flollop back to our room and tell the girlies to go to the beach without me. I can't put my poor pink stomach in the sun again. "I need to go to sleep, anyway," I tell them. "I hardly slept at all last night. I think I need to lie down."

"Poor you," says Mercedes. "Here, I'll pull the blinds down so that it's nice and cool and dark for you."

"Shall I give you some of my Rescue Remedy?" asks Portia. "I'm sure it would help."

"You know, Angel," says Minnie, "we don't have to go to the beach at all. Why don't we all stay here with you?"

"No, no," I say. "You must all go. I'll be fine." Quite honestly, I would much rather be on my own. I just need to lie here and think about things and try to figure out what to do.

They leave reluctantly, promising to bring me back all the seaside gossip at lunchtime. When they're gone, I lie like a beached whale. My head's spinning. There seem to be so many questions that I can't answer.

I hear Potty shout to Maria and Flossie that it's time they were off to the market. "Got to do our ice creamio trials today," he bellows. "We've got twenty-five different flavors to savor . . . come on!"

"And I must go and see Mr. Fruity-Men-Oh-No," shouts Flossie. "He said he'd have some fresh peaches this morning." She chuckles and says, "He told me their skin was just as soft as mine. Ooooh, he is a caution!"

I hear Maria shout, *"Andiamo . . ."* and the front door slams.

Everything is still and quiet and hot. I must have drifted off to sleep for a while, because suddenly I'm awakened by noises coming from the terrace. Maybe it's Antoooownio, deadheading the roses. As the sight of his gorgeous, Latin bod always lifts my spirits, I drag myself out of bed and over to the window. It isn't Antonio, it's Mother. She's sitting at the table, drinking a tiny cup of coffee and smiling to herself. Unseen, I stare at her to see whether she'll give something away about her love affair. But she doesn't do anything more exciting or revealing than finish her coffee and gaze at the garden for a while. Suddenly I have a terrible thought: what if she's waiting for Antonio?? No, that CAN'T be right! I watch, hardly breathing, feeling almost *certain* that Antonio will come around the corner at any moment and wrap Mother up in a passionate embrace. That would be REVOLTING. But, no, nothing happens.

so is this

these are new

131

I go on watching. My heart's thumping as Mother opens her bag and puts on her lipstick. Then she clicks the bag shut and gets up. She's going out again, I think. I must FOLLOW her . . .

I quickly pull on my much-too-hot jeans and one of Mercedes's T-shirts, as I have nothing else to wear. I try to be as quiet as possible, so Mother won't know that I'm there. I hear the front door open and dart like a shadow to the door—well, okay, more like an elephant—and peek out. Mother is climbing into the back seat of the SUV. Eduardo is at the wheel. I can't let her escape—I must see where she is going. But HOW?

In a blinding flash, I know what to do. I bound out through the back door to the garden and find Antonio watering the flowers outside the kitchen. I wave my arms about and say, "Mother, Mother," over and over. Then I make a noise like a motorbike and point to Antonio, point to myself and then make the motorbike noise again.

Antonio stares at me for a few seconds and I feel sure that he doesn't understand. I'm about to get tearful when he says, "You want me to take you on the back of my bike and follow yer old dear, right?"

"Whaaaa . . . ?" I say, with my mouth gaping like a trout. "You speak English?"

"You're havin' a laugh! Course I do—born in the East End of London, I was . . . Now then, I'll just nip up and get my keys and we'll be off . . . Don't worry, darlin'," he says, "I don't ask no questions, me. I just do what the punters want." And then he's gone.

Well, ring my chimes, I think. Fancy that. Antonio bounds

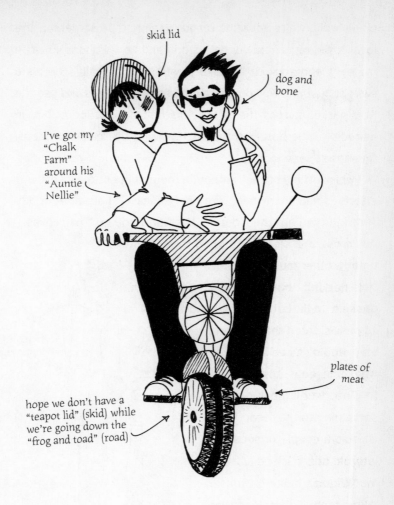

back and before you can say "Bow bells" I'm on the back of his bike, crash helmet down over my ears (SO unflattering) and we're off.

I AM TERRIFIED. Antonio may speak like a Londoner, but he drives like an Italian. He doesn't wear a helmet, and at one point, while we're whizzing through the narrow streets of the local town, he is actually on his dog and bone (phone). I close my eyes and stick to him like plastic wrap. Finally, there's a swirl of dust and we come to a halt. I open my eyes and see the SUV parked across the street, in front of what looks like an incredibly chic hotel. Mother is teetering up the hotel steps. She hasn't seen us.

I whisk off my helmet, without a thought about the disastrous effect it's had on my hair. "Wait here, please," I hiss to Antonio.

"Right you are then, darlin'. Mind how you go," he replies.

I cross the street and walk toward the hotel. Mother mustn't see me.

I needn't have worried. Mother doesn't look behind her, and she's so near-sighted that she prob-ably wouldn't see me, any-way. She goes straight up to the front desk, says something to the reception-ist, and a couple of seconds later a tall, dark, devastat-ingly good-looking white-suited man arrives. He smiles a sparkling smile at Mother and ushers her . . . UPSTAIRS!!

this must be Filippo—he looks so smooth he could slide uphill

I stand there, gawking, SURE that I'm going

to faint. I'm so hot . . . the room is going round and round . . . Oh no, I don't think I'm going to fall down—I think I'm going to throw up . . .

"*Signorina*?" a voice comes to me through the waves of ickyness, and a glass of cool, lemony drink is put in my hand. "Please," the voice says and I take a sip. "*Va bene*," says the voice of my ministering angel and all at once I know that I'm not going to puke all over this beautiful room, after all. I smile at the pretty waitress who has saved me from shame, and stumble out of the building.

I'm blinded by tears and am almost squashed by a passing Ferrari, as I cross the road. I'm sobbing by the time I reach Antonio.

why would I care if I'm squashed by a Ferrari?

"What's up, doll?" he asks, handing me his hanky. "Shall I take you back to Alfie's gaff? Come on, climb aboard. No need for the waterworks. I'll get you back and then you can have a nice cup of tea."

"Okay," I sob, knowing that it's going to take a lot more than a cup of tea to put things right.

We zoom back through the streets to Alfie"s "gaff." I arrive feeling drenched with misery and heat, and badly needing a shower and something to eat. A little comfort of the JONC, Superstar variety would not be amiss. I thank Antonio for being my knight on a white charger—well, man on a red motor-bike, actually—and fumble my way in through the front door of the villa.

The girlies must be back from the beach, because I can hear voices and splashing sounds coming from the pool. That's funny, I think: they don't usually go down to the pool after they've been on the beach. Perhaps Dynamo Dweeb was being a pain and they decided to come back early. There are two big backpacks in the hall with stuff spilling out of them. One of them looks familiar, but I can't remember where I last saw it . . . I stagger out to the pool and, as I come out of the shade of the house, for a moment I'm blinded by the bright sunlight.

"YOO HOO!" shouts Minnie, from the water, waving her arms around. "Angel, where have you been? LOOK WHO'S HERE!!"

# Blush-Pink Cooler

*35 oz. (approx. 9 cups)
raspberries, fresh or frozen
11 oz. (3 cups) red currants,
stalks removed
(You can substitute cranberries.)
¾ cup mineral water
sugar syrup (see below)
ice cubes*

*pretty sprigs of mint or
lemon balm to garnish.*

*SUGAR SYRUP
4½ cups water
4½ cups sugar*

---

Before you can make this divine drink, you need to make some
sugar syrup. It's really easy. Put the water and the sugar in
a saucepan. Bring the mixture to the boil and stir it until all the
sugar has dissolved. Let the syrup cool before pouring it into a
clean container. Cover it and store it in the fridge until you
need to use it. Sugar syrup will keep for a long time in the
fridge and will be there whenever you need to make a refreshing
little something to knock back when you're feeling frazzled.

Put the raspberries in the blender and purée. Strain the purée
through a sieve into a pitcher. Repeat with the red currants or
cranberries. Pour the juice into the pitcher with the raspberry
juice. Add the mineral water to the juice mixture along with as
much sugar syrup as you like (it depends how sweet you want it).
Pour it into a tall glass filled with ice. Pop a sprig of greenery on
the top for a dead sophisticated "cocktail." SO revitalizing!

Makes enough to share with 3 friends.

## chapter fourteen

# Golden Gobsmacker

**I'M STILL SQUINTING** into the sunlight when what appears to be a glorioso body rises out of the swimming pool and waves at me. "Come on in, Angel," says a familiar voice. "It's fantastic."

I stare as the tall, golden-limbed, and strikingly good-looking boy comes toward me. He's grinning at me and suddenly my eyes become used to the light and I realize . . . it's GEORGE!! GOOD GRIEF! IT IS GEORGE! But what's happened to him? He's all tanned and lean and blond and PHWOOOOAR!!!

But hang on, what's happening to ME? This is old, familiar George, who used to cry if his Ready Brek was too hot. So why is my stomach doing backflips and my mouth hanging open like Mother's wallet at Harrods' summer sale?

"How are you, Angel?" says George, planting the coolest swimming-pool-fresh kiss on my cheek. "The others said you weren't feeling well. Are you okay now?"

"I'm fine," I say. "Back in a minute . . ." And I scuttle as fast as I can back into the villa. I can't face George looking like this. I must smell horrid and my face is all smudged from the

tears and my hair is all squashed from the crash helmet. I need time to get my head together.

As I get up-close-and-personal with the soap on a rope, and try to get the tangles out of my hair, I wonder *why* George is here. And while I'm wondering, a tiny thought starts jumping up and down in the back of my mind so that I can't ignore it.

When I first saw the backpacks in the hall, I thought for the teensiest, most fleeting moment that Sydney had come to see me, and almost as swiftly I felt my heart sink. I haven't really given Sydney a thought over the past few days and I have to admit to myself (although I wouldn't DREAM of admitting it to anyone else), that deep down I don't really, honestly, truthfully miss him . . . In fact, I don't think I feel anything much for him anymore.

My life has gone completely pear-shaped. Not only that, but now that my pear-shaped body is squeaky clean, I don't know what clothes to put it in. I can't wear my bikini with my bright, red tummy, but I haven't got anything else. I want to lie by the pool with the others. Oh, KNICKERS!

I know, I think, I'll pop up to Flossie's room and see if her swimsuit is anywhere around. I know she won't mind if I borrow it.

Flossie's room is a riot of color and such a mess, with clothes all over the place and a huge vase of flowers and bowls of fruit cluttering the surfaces. Flossie "abroad" is certainly very different from Flossie at home.

I find the bathing suit poking out from under an amazing red, satin dress that surely can't be Flossie's. I haven't got time to wonder about it because I'm suddenly desperate to see George, to find out what he's doing here and to talk to him about Mother.

Seeing him today, I wonder if I had been a bit hasty when I told George ages ago that we couldn't be boyfriend and girlfriend because I thought of him as a brother. I do, in a way, because we've grown up together. But I don't think I could have properly looked at him until just then . . . and he has always been nice to me (except when he was being horrid about Sydney . . . but now I think that he might have been right about that particular person, after all).

I pull on the bathing suit and look at myself in the mirror. Although Flossie is as round as a pea, it's quite tight and there are white pudding basin things hanging out at the front.

There's a lot of my bottom
hanging out at the back too,
but at least it's tanned . . .
Then I realize that the pudding basins should be on
the INSIDE. I tuck them
in and find that they
keep my boobs in
place, which is a relief.

I don't think the
bathing suit's ever been
worn and actually it's not
at all bad. It's navy blue with
a white band around the top.
The color is quite slimming and
the white band makes my brown
bits look even browner.

St. Michael, whose name I saw in
the back of the suit, must really
be the patron saint of
swimwear. I borrow Portia's

*I suppose
these could
be some sort
of swimming
aid, like
armbands?*

*a bit tight
round the
rear*

sparkly shoes—the ones I wore to the cocktail party, give my
hair a quick flick, pull in my tummy, and go back to the pool.

They're all lying out in the sun when I reappear, looking like
Miss United Kingdom circa 1960. (I only need a sash and a tiara
and you would never know the difference.) I notice for the first
time that there is another boy here too. It's Jimmie! I look over
to Minnie. Yes, she looks adorably adoring.

141

"Come and sit down, Angel," says George, leaping up as I sashay around the pool. "Are you okay?"

"Yes," I say. "But what on earth are you doing here?"

"Oh, we were . . . er . . . just passing through, so we thought we'd drop in!" He's grinning at me and it really is quite disturbing how wonderful he looks.

I try to get my mind back into gear. "Don't be daft," I say. "You don't just pass through Italy on your way back from the West Indies. Even I know that, and I barely passed my geography exam last term."

"Well," he says, "we thought you would all be missing us and that it would be nice for you if we turned up."

"I think you're completely nuts, but it *is* good to see you . . .

does he have to just sit there looking all golden and gorgeous?

why doesn't my hair go stripy-blond in the sun?

boys are so lucky—they never have to worry about having gorilla legs

both," I say, giving Jimmie a little wave. "But listen, George," I hiss, getting down close to his ear. "I HAVE to speak to you. There have been some very fishy things going on here."

"Fishy, eh?" says George, doing his raised-eyebrow thing. Then he smiles and, for the first time, I notice that he's got dimples that are almost as good as the ones Mr. Dreamy Dimples, the divine (married) chef from Greatsnott, has . . .

"Yes," I say, quickly trying to pull myself together. "I need to talk to you . . . ALONE . . ."

"This is not about Saddo Sydney, I hope," says George as he follows me into the living room.

"Who? Oh no. No, it's much more important than that."

"Anything would be," says George. "Have you heard from him?"

"No," I say. "Do shut up about him and listen . . ."

I give him the lowdown on Mother. All about how suspiciously she's been acting. I finish up with the details of my visit to the hotel this morning and say, "So, you see, Mother MUST be having an affair . . ."

I wait for George to explode into uncontrolled disbelief and anger. But what does he do?

HE JUST SMILES . . . (Admittedly it's one of those rather sweet, dimply smiles . . . but still . . .)

"Don't you care?" I shout.

But before he can answer, we hear the front door open, and Mother calls, "Hellooo . . . Anyone at home?"

"We're in here," I shout back to her. I whisper to George, "She's going to have a fit when she sees you here . . ."

Mother wafts in. She stops for a second and looks at us then SHE SMILES TOO!

143

She comes forward, gives George a kiss and says, "How are you, dahling?" for all the world as if she were expecting him.

"I'm fine" he says, kissing her back. "Jimmie's outside with the other girls."

"Good," says Mother.

Good? What does she mean, "Good"? Doesn't she mean "Why have you come here, and brought your friend with you, when you are supposed to be going back to London?"

But she doesn't say anything like that. Instead, she settles herself down on the pale leather sofa and says, "Now that you're here, there's something I want to ask you, George, dahling. Angel's been having such a beastly time recently that it would be lovely if you would take her to Coco's in town and help her choose a beautiful dress. She doesn't appear to have brought any clothes with her and she needs a little something to take her mind off that Sydney person and cheer her up. Do you think you could do that for me?"

"Certainly," says George and they both turn to me and smile.

I'm amazed. Since when has Mother noticed that I have been brokenhearted? She's never mentioned Sydney before. Is this a bribe? Perhaps the dress is a bribe to stop me from telling Potty about her sordid affair. But why did George laugh when I told HIM? Why is everyone on Mother's side?

I DON'T UNDERSTAND. I can't think why Potty doesn't see what Mother is doing. How come he looks happy all the time when she's hardly here at all? Is he blind? I know he's batty, but I never thought he was stupid.

WHAT IS GOING ON?

\* \* \*

Supper is a riot. Even though I feel dizzier and more confused than a hamster on its wheel, I can't help enjoying myself. Everyone is in such good spirits. George and Jimmie tell really funny stories about their vacation and Minnie is flirting with Jimmie for all she's worth. It's working, of course. No boy in his right mind could resist Minnie, full flirt (except George, of course, but then George's mind isn't always right). Maria, Flossie, and Potty have brought back fantastic foody things from the market. There's so much food—more than enough for everyone.

Potty is properly amazed to see George and Jimmie. "Golly," he says, "how fantastic that you two happened to be passing . . . What a coincidence you showing up here! Clarissa, did you know anything about this?"

Mother shakes her head and says, "I think it's wonderful of them to make the effort to come all the way over here. It's fabulous, dahlings, to see you both."

So Potty obviously wasn't expecting George and Jimmie, and maybe Mother wasn't, either. I'm puzzled about why she wasn't more surprised to see George, but then I remember that, surprise is another facial expression mother thinks is aging.

Potty starts practicing his Italian on Maria, and Flossie, who is looking quite sunburned, is telling us all about how wonderful Mr. Fruity-Men-Oh-No has been. "He's found me all manner of unusualities," she says. I notice that her hair isn't done up quite as tightly this evening.

Mother looks calm and happy and I wonder what sort of person she can be to cheerfully mess up this wonderful vaction with her Low-Life Latin Lover.

I put off going to bed—I'm so worried that I'll have another

sleepless night. So much has happened and my head is full of questions without any answers . . .

But when I do finally go to bed, I fall into the deepest sleep, and dream that I am dancing with St. Michael. He's wonderful and I feel SO contented. I feel as if I've met him before somewhere, and when I look at him again he's turned into George.

# Tabby Fat Cats

*(sometimes known as Golden Flapjacks)*

1 stick butter
4 tbsp golden syrup (same color as George's hair)
1 rounded tbsp soft dark brown sugar

1 tbsp raisins
1 tbsp mixed nuts, chopped
⅓ cup dried cherries, chopped
2⅚ cups oatmeal

---

Heat the oven to 350°. Grease an 8-inch-square cake pan, or line it with parchment paper.

Put the butter, syrup, and sugar in a saucepan and melt over a low heat. When the butter has melted and the sugar has dissolved, remove the pan from the heat and stir in the remaining ingredients.

Press the mixture into the prepared pan and bake in the oven for 20 to 25 minutes.

Take the fat cat out of the oven and cut it into 14 bars while it is still warm.

## chapter fifteen

# Shops, Shoes, and Secret Secrets

**I DON'T REALLY** want to go to this oh-so-smart shop called Coco, but I don't want to argue with Mother, either, so I agree to go and choose something. I ask the girlies to come with us. I can't go on my own with George—now that he's gone deeply devastating, it would all be too embarrassing.

"Golly!" says Minnie. "You are just SO lucky! My mum would never send me off to a really expensive shop and just tell me to 'buy something' like that. You can have anything you want."

What I want is for Mother to stop doing what she's doing, but even though I would usually tell my friends everything, I'm in such a muddle I don't think I can explain any of it to Minnie just yet.

"You really are lucky," sighs Portia. "After my mum's had this baby I don't expect there will be any money for me to have ANY clothes at all."

I know Portia's suffering from shock, so I won't point out that as both her parents are highly paid medical specialists, it's unlikely that she'll have to go around dressed in rags after the baby's born.

Portia rang her mum a few days ago and asked her straight out if she was pregnant. Her mum said she was and that she was sorry she hadn't told Portia sooner, but she'd wanted to be sure that everything was all right before telling everyone. We all think it's so exciting, but Portia isn't convinced. She thinks that she will have to spend all her time babysitting and doesn't fancy the idea of being puked over, or of having to go anywhere near anything resembling a diaper. EW! She was too young when her little sisters were babies to do anything as responsible as babysitting or diaper changing.

By the time we are all ready for our shopping spree, it's nearly 11 A.M. and Flossie is already making a start on Jamie O's sublime, pukka, blinding, fish with pancetta. I want to stay and help her. I feel safe in the kitchen, especially when we're "doing a Jamie." I haven't done nearly as much cooking during the holiday as I had hoped I would. Flossie and Maria have taken over the kitchen and they have enough trouble with Potty pottering around doing his "tastings" without me in there too.

I'm thinking of asking Flossie if I can help her, when George comes in. "Come on," he says, all bright and beautiful, "let's go and outfit you."

"I'm not a soldier," I say. "I don't need outfitting."

But he smiles at me and my feet switch to autopilot and follow him out of the door. The girlies are right behind us.

Coco's isn't at all the sort of shop you should go to in swim-suits and wraps, but that's what we girls are wearing. The boys are dead scruffy in shorts and T-shirts. It's fearfully chic in here and when the shop assistant looks me up and down and says, "And what can we do for you?" I feel a bit like Julia Roberts in *Pretty Woman*.

The girlies send the boys to sit in the square while they help me choose a dress. I do a lot of prancing around in different designs (quite a few of which, unkindly, refuse to zip up–Italian sizes are minuscule compared to British ones). Minnie gives me fashion advice in between frequent longing looks out the shop door at Jimmie.

I end up with the most fab frock. It's low cut and floaty with one of those handkerchief-point hems. It's Italian size gigantic, but, with all the swimming I've been doing, I'm hardly wobbling at all these days. And besides, what does it matter what it says on the label as long as it looks good? It's deep violet and I LOVE it. I don't know when I'll ever wear it, but Mercedes says that perhaps we could organize a posh dinner at Alfie's villa before we all go home and then I would get a chance to wear my dress. Portia says I must get shoes to match, and the shop has a pair of strappy sandals that are overwhelmingly elegant and match the dress perfectly. They make me look very tall, but I can't resist them.

so high they make my legs go on for miles and they hardly hurt at all

My friends are so lovely. They don't mind a bit that they are not buying beautiful dresses themselves, but I must say I feel quite embarrassed by how much all this is going to cost.

When the dress and the shoes are all packed up beautifully, we shout for George to come and hand over Mother's money.

Annoyingly, I have to admit that Mother is right—the shopping trip has cheered me up a bit. There's something so exciting about a smart shopping bag with oceans of white tissue paper and a posh frock nestling inside it. And as for a new shoebox, well . . . But although I don't feel as miserable as before, I don't feel any better about Mother. It wouldn't matter how many dresses she bought me, I still couldn't forgive her for what she's doing.

Before heading home, we go to a café for cappuccinos, which Minnie insists on calling "cow-poo-in-yer-nose", and just a tiny ice cream, or two. When we get back to the villa, Mother is in her room. I can hear her singing. She's probably been with "him" all morning and that's why she's so happy. I go upstairs to show her the dress and to thank her. I don't know why, but my knees are trembling.

Minnie fluttering over the foam

"Dahling," she gushes as I walk in, "how did you do? Did you find some divine little number, something you feel *molto elegante* in?"

I can't stand to hear her speak Italian now that I know she only learned it so that she could speak to "him."

I show her the dress and she fingers the beautiful fabric. "*Bella, bellissima!* I bet my little Angel looks *fabuloso* in this," she says, pulling the dress out of the bag.

Mother's really good at unpacking shopping— she's had loads of practice

"Please, Mother," I say, "don't speak Italian. I know why you do it."

Mother looks puzzled, but now that I've begun I take a deep breath, clench my bottom and carry on. "It's all right, Mother. I'm a woman of the world . . ." I gulp as Mother looks more and more perplexed. "I know about LOVE. You can confide in me . . . I'll try to understand. I already know about Filippo."

Mother roars with laughter (which, as I've already mentioned, is really unusual for her, as "Laugh lines are only for comedians"). She leans forward and gives me a hug. "Dahling," she splutters, "Filippo is my Italian teacher in London. And if you saw him, dahling, you would understand why I'm laughing." She mops the tears of laughter from her eyes. "Oh, sweetheart, don't look so miserable. I can see I shall have to come clean."

I hold my breath and wait for the bombshell.

Mother sits down and opens her mouth to speak. There's a

pause and then she begins. "I'd been feeling for some time that my life was rather . . . well, rather worthless. After Potty's trial I began to wonder why it had taken a terrible incident like that to make me do something helpful for someone else. I just felt . . . oh, I don't know . . . that having beauty treatments and going shopping wasn't much of a way to spend my life. I really enjoyed being of use to Potty. I'd had to use my brain a bit and, you know, I found that I could. I realized that I had a brain, and that I was wasting it doing nothing, but shopping. SO . . ." Mother pauses and looks at me, I feel myself getting shivery, despite the heat, "I decided that I would learn to speak Italian so that I could organize a surprise party in Italy to celebrate our silver wedding anniversary. You know how much Potty loves Italy, and when dahling Alfie offered us the use of his villa, I thought 'Right! This is the perfect opportunity.' Dahling, I know how hopelessly sweet you are about never being able to keep anything from him, so I didn't want you to know."

I'm stunned. "So you've been learning Italian so that you could organize a surprise party for Potty?" I gasp.

"That's right, dahling."

HOW FABULOUS!

"But what about the incredibly handsome man I happened to see you with at the hotel?" I ask.

"You silly goose," answers Mother. "That was Signor Martini. He's the manager of the hotel . . . Dahling, you didn't think that Mumsy was having an affair with him, did you? And what were you doing at the hotel anyway?"

"I followed you," I whine. "I needed to know who you were

seeing, and when I saw that man take you upstairs, I thought . . .
I thought . . ."

"Good heavens! Angel, how could you? Signor Martini was showing me the glorious ballroom on the first floor. It has views over the sea and is completely beautiful . . . How could you possibly think that I would have an affair—and with HIM? If you knew him, you would realize that Signor Martini would never seduce a WOMAN. And anyway, why would I want to have an affair, when I've got Potty?"

I can't answer that. My eyes are brimming over with tears, but they're happy tears. That's the sweetest thing I've ever heard Mother say.

Suddenly I remember George.

"George knew?" I say, sniffling.

"Well, I had to make sure that he would be here," Mother answers.

"And Flossie?" I ask, as pieces of the puzzle begin to plop into place.

"Dahling," replies Mother, "I had to have SOME help!"

"OOOOOH!" I sigh. As Mother gives me a great big hug, I feel as if the weight of the world has been lifted from my shoulders. Honestly, I'd forgotten what it felt like to be hugged by Mother—she's all warm and smells beautiful of something flowery and expensive. It's lovely!

"That's why you needed a dress," she says.

"Oh," I snivel, "that is such, such good news! I was so worried that you and Potty were breaking up . . . Oh, Mother!" I wail as she hugs me again.

When I've calmed down a little, I suddenly have another

thought, "Oooooooh!" I sniff hard. "Did the girlies know about the party all the time?"

"No," says Mother. "I didn't want anyone to let the cat out of the bag."

"Wow!" I gasp. "Imagine you keeping all this secret and me not guessing what was going on."

"Well," says Mother, all serious, "if I had thought it would make you so worried and unhappy, I would never have kept anything from you. But, dahling, now that you *do* know, be a cutesie wootsie, won't you, and DON'T TELL POTTY . . ."

## chapter sixteen

# Party Time and Everything's Fine (Or Is It?)

IMAGINE MOTHER thinking that I wouldn't be able to keep Potty's surprise party a secret! Of course I can keep a secret . . . It's just that knowing something SO exciting, and seeing Potty and knowing that he doesn't know what I know, and knowing that Mother has known for ages what I know now is making me feel quite GIDDY.

BUT I HAVEN'T SAID A WORD.

I nearly did, though, when Potty asked me why I was practicing my dance steps in the kitchen. I said, "Because of the paaaa . . ." remembering just in time that I musn't give it away and changing "party" to "parasites", which was the first thing that came into my head. "Because of the paaarasites," I said. "I'm trying to stamp on all these BEASTLY parasites!" I'm not sure Potty believed me; he gave me a very funny look. I was BURSTING to tell him. Every time I saw him after that I had to hurtle off in the other direction. Poor Potty, I think he was quite upset.

* * *

It's the day of the party, and luckily Potty is busy writing a report for Alfie. It's called "Olives I Have Known and Loved" and it's giving the rest of us a chance to get on with "arrangements" for the evening.

The girlies are trying on their outfits. Mother agreed that I could let them in on the secret—I couldn't keep it from them!

I would look happier if all boys weren't such WORMS

this dress is creamy white, simple, and stonkingly stunning

corset bit round Portia's middle

cutesie-wootsie, homemade glam frock

doesn't often wear skirts—she says she's got thick ankles, but actually it's just that the rest of her is so thin . . .

"I bet you dance with George tonight, Angel," giggles Minnie. "I've seen you gazing at him."

"And I bet you dance with Jimmie," I say, not really wanting to discuss George, ". . . and Portia, you will dance with Jack, I know Mother won't mind if you invite him . . . who will you dance with, Mercedes?" I ask, suddenly feeling worried about her.

"Oh, I'll be fine," she says.

"Well, it's not as if every other boy in the room wouldn't dance with you if you would only let them," says Portia.

"Yeah," says Minnie, "or Angel could lend you one of the gorgeous Italian Stallions who keep chatting her up."

Mercedes smiles. "I'll have a lovely time," she says, "and I'll tell Paul all about it when I get home."

"Aaaaah!" the rest of us sigh together.

"Do you think your mother has invited Mr. PPP?" giggles Minnie. "She might know him."

"Crumbs, I hope not," I say. "What do you think he would wear to a party? Diamond-studded crotch huggers, or black leather buttock crunchers?"

"Definitely, buttock crunchers, but perhaps with a padded posing pouch over the top?" suggests Portia as she collapses, wheezing with laughter, onto her bed.

"And his shirt open to the waist," snorts Mercedes. "And a chest wig and fifteen medallions . . ."

"Enough!" I squeak. "We've got more important things to think about than Mr. PPP, like, what color lippy am I going to wear?"

"But seriously, Angel," says Minnie, wiping her eyes with

her T-shirt, "who is coming? Do you know?"

"Mother told me that she's invited friends from all over the place and that people have been flying in since yesterday. They're all staying at the really chic hotel where I saw Mother and her 'lover'." (I told the girlies that I thought Mother was having an affair—I can laugh about it now.)

I can hardly believe how great and groovy I feel today. It's as if all the ducks of despair on my shoulders have suddenly flown away. What do I care if Saddo Syd doesn't love having me love him? He doesn't know what he's missing and he'll be truly, madly, deeply sorry when he finds out.

I still can't get over the fact that Mother would learn to speak Italian *just* so that she could arrange the perfect party for Potty. It's just so PUKKA. I sometimes think I hardly know Mother at all. She can be seriously surprising.

Everyone is busy with last-minute preparations for this evening. Mother and Flossie are at the hotel seeing that the flowers are right and that the food is going to be perfect and that the band has arrived.

George and Jimmie are in town collecting their rented dinner suits, and Antonio and Maria are on patrol. They're under strict instructions to make sure that Potty doesn't suspect a thing if he finishes his report before Mother gets back.

Mother is going to tell him that she is taking him out to dinner as a last-night-of-the-holiday treat. She's hoping that this will encourage him to wear the right sort of clothes, but, knowing Potty, he'll probably put on his favorite pajama trousers with a checked jacket on top. I expect he'll wear his panama hat too.

We all have to get to the hotel before them, so we've made a cunning plan with Eduardo. He will meet us round the back of the villa and take us into town first, then come back for Mother and Potty.

I can't wait to put on my gobsmackingly gorgeous gown. I've hung it up in my room with the shoes underneath it, so that I can admire it from every angle. I can imagine how it will feel when I drift into the fabulous ballroom at the hotel, with my skirt all swirling and curling round my legs.

I decide to take a bath in the huge bathtub. I think I'll put in some of that delish smelly stuff that Mother uses . . .

The door bangs and interrupts my train of thought.

"Hiya," says George as he bounds past our room. I follow him to the room he and Jimmie are sharing and watch him hang up his posh rented suit.

"You'll never guess who we met in town, Angel," he says.

"Who?" I ask, noticing that George's hair is just long enough at the back to begin curling over his collar . . . sweet.

"Melissa . . . Do you remember her?"

"Not really," I say, remembering full well. She was that bimbo that George was so besotted with when he was about fifteen. Her dad's an awesomely wealthy banker. "Mel" (or Smelly Melly, as I used to call her) had frothy blonde curls and teeth like tombstones and an amazing figure. I LOATHED her.

"Well, she's a girl I used to know, and it was so great to see her that I invited her to come tonight," explains George.

"You did WHAT?" I yelp.

"I invited her to Potty's surprise party. We dropped in at the hotel on the way back and asked your mother if it was all right.

She said it would be marvelous and that she would put Melissa next to me at dinner," says George, grinning.

Jimmie's smiling too, and I want to slap them both and wipe the stupid, cheesy grins off their suntanned faces.

"Great, isn't it! She said she was really looking forward to seeing you again, so that'll be wicked, won't it?" says George breezily.

"Yeah . . . wicked," I say, as I lift my chin up off the floor and shuffle back to my bedroom.

I lie on my bed all afternoon with my eyes shut. The others think I'm asleep, so they creep around, trying not to disturb me. I'm not asleep. I'm thinking over and over again how much I hate boys, and willing Melissa to go into meltdown before this evening. I try to kid myself that if I wish for it hard enough, she'll go up in a puff of smoke, like the Wicked Witch of the West. Not that I care about George being with her. I couldn't care less what George is up to. He's welcome to Smelly Melly. I just don't want her at Potty's party. She'll spoil everything.

"Come on, Angel," says Mercedes, gently shaking my shoulder. "It's time to get ready. You've been asleep for ages . . . you're going to be sparkling tonight!"

"Yeah," I say, sitting up, "whatever."

The others are all so busy getting into their party gear that they don't notice how bummed out I am. Mind you, just before we go to meet Eduardo, Portia does point out that I'm wearing my flip-flops instead of my posh shoes.

"What's up, babes?" she asks. "Aren't you feeling well?"

"As well as can be expected," I say grouchily, putting on my shoes.

"Come on," she says, "you mustn't be blue about Sydney . . . Here, let me help you with your hair," she flicks up my hair with her curling iron. "You look sooooperb," she says, giving me a hug. "Don't be sad at Potty's party—it'll spoil it for him."

I seem to have done so much moaning about my problems, my family, and my boyfriend (ex) recently that I can't bring myself to tell Portia that I haven't been thinking about Sydney for ages, or that Mouthy Melissa is the cause of my misery, or even that I suppose I might, in my heart of hearts, be a tiny bit sad that George will be otherwise engaged all evening. I realize, though, that she is absolutely right. This is Potty and Mother's evening. I must try to be happy.

"You're right, babes," I say, twirling round on my sophisticated sandals before lashing on the lippy. "Let's go!"

The boys (both of whom, I decide, are COMPLETE RATS) have already left for the hotel. They borrowed Antonio's motorbike because they thought that would be totally cool (how SAD) and I expect they have already met Mouthy Melissa and that George is all over her like a rash. (UGH!)

We're outside the villa, cleverly concealed from view of the upstairs windows, waiting for Eduardo to fetch the SUV, when Flossie appears. CREAMY CUPCAKES!!! WHAT'S HAPPENED TO FLOSSIE?? Her hair is all loose and curly, and she's wearing the red, satin dress I saw in her room. IT'S STRAPLESS!! In the front of the dress she has pinned a huge, red rose. She's wearing MAKEUP and sparkly, dangly earrings!

162

*what can I say?
frock 'em dead,
Flossie!*

"WOW, Flossie!" we four say in unison. "You look AMAZING!"

"Well," she says, tossing her curls, "a body's got to make the most of themself—that's what Maria says and I think she's absolutely right. As my grandmother used to say, 'If you've got it, flaunt it!' So I thought I would! And besides Mr. Fruity-Men-Oh-No likes a woman to look like a woman . . ." (I wonder to myself what Diggory would think.)

"I don't think there would be any mistaking you for anything other than a woman, tonight," I say.

"I think we all look a picture," says Flossie. "Now come on, girls," she says, as Eduardo pulls up in the SUV, "we must be off."

When we arrive in the awesomely beautiful ballroom on the first floor of the hotel I look around for Melissa, but I can't see her anywhere. The place is full of people and I assume she and George are pawing each other in some dark corner. Jimmie's here, though. He and Dynamo Dweeb (who turns out to be the saddo son of one of Mother's friends) make a dash for Minnie as soon as she comes in. Jimmie makes short work of Dweeb telling him to "Go back to the nursery and leave us grown-ups in peace." (I think this is really cruel, but typical of the sort of person who would be friends with rat-face, weasel-breath . . . gloriously tanned and dimpled George.)

Flossie waves to her Fruity Man and dashes off to join him, just as Signor Martini signals to us that Mother and Potty are arriving. The whole room goes quiet. So quiet you could hear a mouse hiccup. Everyone is still. Then we hear Potty bellowing as he and Mother come up the stairs, "I say, old thing, this is all jolly fabaroooni!" Everyone tries not to laugh. And then, there they are . . . standing at the top of the steps that lead into the ballroom.

Suddenly everyone is shouting "Surprise!" and throwing rose petals.

Mother and Potty look fantastic. Mother is dressed from head to toe in beaded Armani and Potty is wearing full evening dress with a pink rose in his buttonhole! He grins and grins as he looks around the room at all his friends. Then he makes a sign for us all to be quiet.

"I want to say a few little words to my darling wife," he says.

We all wait, holding our breath, to hear what he will say.

He doesn't *say* anything. He goes down on one knee and looks up at Mother. Then he SINGS to her in ITALIAN, before presenting her with a small, black leather box that HAS to contain something sparkly.

I'm filling up! Potty must have guessed what was going on. That's why he's got the present and why he's wearing the right clothes. Mother could have told me, after all. Potty must have known all along.

Everyone cheers, and looking around, I can see that there isn't a dry eye in the house. Even Mother, who doesn't do facial expressions, dabs at her eyes, before giving Potty a kiss.

"Angel," says a voice at my shoulder, "you look amazing!" I turn around and see George standing beside me.

"Oh!" I say, looking over his shoulder. "So where's Melissa?" I expect she's gone to put her lipstick back on, now that George has sucked it all off. Or maybe she's gone to check that her dress is tight enough, so that we can all see her fantastic (not) body. Or perhaps she's waiting for George to do his family duty and then get back to her. I don't want him to be talking to me because he thinks it's his DUTY.

"She's not here," he says. "I didn't meet her this morning and even if I had I would never have invited her . . . she was rough." Seeing my expression, he goes on, "It was meant to be a joke and I kind of wanted to see if you would care . . ."

"Oh!" I gush. "That is SO sweet . . . and SO MEAN . . . How could you do that to me? PIG!" But I can't help smiling and then I can't help laughing. And the whole room seems to be laughing too.

After the most totally scrummy yummy dinner, the dancing begins. Jack has joined us after dinner, and he scoops Portia up into a little wannabe-doctors huddle. Jimmie and Minnie are cheek to cheerful cheek, and Mercedes is teaching some of Potty and Mother's friends how to make some modern moves on the dance floor.

Fruity-Man-Oh-No

"Looks like you're going to have to dance with me, then," says George.

"Okay," I say. "If I must!" We move on to the dance floor. I feel so happy. I don't have to try to be anything different with George. He knows me so well. I can just be myself.

"So, is Saddo Syd history, then?" asks George.

"Yeah," I say, knowing that it's true and not minding in the least.

"Will you be sending ME a year's supply of Love Hearts?"

"How did you know about that?" I gasp.

"Oh, a little bird told me."

Across the floor, we can see Flossie and her Fruity Man doing a fandango. Flossie has her rose between her teeth, and is tossing her curls as they dance cheek to cheek.

"Well!" I say, "some truly weird things have happened on this holiday, and that's for sure . . . Flossie's had a Mediterranean makeover, and look . . ." I point to the balcony. "Mother and Potty . . . I was convinced they were breaking up, but look at them!" George turns and we both watch Mother and Potty, who are holding hands and gazing out at the ocean, together.

"So," says George, looking deep into my eyes, "everyone's in love—and what about you, Angel?"

"Oh," I say, without a moment's hesitation, "I love Jamie Oliver Naked Chef and Deee . . ." But before I can finish, George stops me talking by engaging my mouth in a quite different activity!